THE GET-AWAY CAR

The
GET-AWAY CAR

by Eleanor Clymer

E. P. Dutton   New York

Library of Congress Cataloging in Publication Data

Clymer, Eleanor Lowenton, date   The get-away car.

SUMMARY: A young girl's grandmother has a knack for
helping people with their problems while simultaneously
solving her own.
[1. Grandmothers—Fiction]   I. Title.
PZ7.C6272Ge   1978   [Fic]   78-7445   ISBN: 0-525-30470-3

Published in the United States by E. P. Dutton, a Division
of Sequoia-Elsevier Publishing Company, Inc., New York

Published simultaneously in Canada by Clarke,
Irwin & Company Limited, Toronto and Vancouver

Editor: Ann Durell   Designer: Lorraine Visconi
Printed in the U.S.A.   First Edition
10 9 8 7 6 5 4 3 2 1

for Jane Emily

ONE

Maggie and Grandma were sitting at the kitchen table. It was Saturday, a beautiful day in June, as Maggie could see by leaning out of the window and craning her neck to look up at the patch of blue sky over the alley. It was a narrow alley between two buildings, and as she leaned out she could hear noises—babies yelling, radios blaring and people arguing.

It was a good day for going somewhere. A whole free weekend stretched ahead of them.

"What shall we do?" Maggie asked.

"Well," Grandma said, wrinkling her forehead as if she were thinking hard, "let's see. There are the clothes to wash. And the house needs cleaning and you have homework."

"No, I don't," said Maggie. "It's the last week of school. They didn't give us any."

"Good. Then you can clean the house," said Grandma. "I'm feeling tired. Guess I'll have another cup of coffee and go back to bed."

"I just remembered I do have homework."

"Oh! Then we can't go for a cookout."

"Were we going for a cookout?"

Grandma and Maggie liked to tease each other.

"Yes, that's why I bought all those hot dogs and marshmallows. But we can eat them at home. We can ask your friends to come and help."

"But Diane thinks we're going to the park," said Maggie.

"Then we better go," said Grandma. "We don't want to disappoint Diane. See if you can reach the coffeepot."

Maggie got up and poured Grandma a cup of coffee. Then she took a doughnut for herself and sat down to munch it. She looked at her grandmother, plump and pink-cheeked, just the picture of what a grandmother ought to be. The kind that knitted sweaters and kept the house tidy.

But Maggie knew better. Grandma's motto was Fun First, Work Later. Maggie liked living with Grandma. She had lived with her since she was five and her parents split up.

She had no other relatives on her mother's side except for one cousin of Grandma's, whom Maggie had seen when she was very small but could hardly remember. On her father's side there was Aunt Ruby Fisher.

When Maggie's mother had gone off in one direction

and her father in another, Grandma had taken Maggie to live with her. Aunt Ruby objected strongly. She came to the apartment and demanded Maggie.

"This place you live in is not fit for a child," she said.

Grandma had retorted: "If it's good enough for me, it's good enough for my grandchild."

Aunt Ruby said that besides that, Grandma went out to work every day, she was too old, didn't know how to feed a child (look at those Pop-Tarts and hot dogs on the table!) and other things.

"And what about you?" Grandma inquired. "How do *you* know what's good for children?"

Aunt Ruby said, "I've read books about nutrition, psychology and education, and I live in a respectable neighborhood. And I can stay home and dedicate myself to raising her."

Grandma thought about it a while. Then she said, "We can argue about it till the cows come home. Maybe we better ask Maggie what she wants."

"How can a child of that age know what she wants?" Aunt Ruby exclaimed.

"I think she can," said Grandma.

Maggie looked from one to the other. Grandma, in a printed cotton housedress, her white hair curling around her face, looked comfortable, the sort of person whose lap you could sit on. Aunt Ruby was tall and skinny, her face creased into a worried frown, her hands clutching a big pocketbook.

What was going to happen? Maggie wondered. Were they going to sit here, talking and talking? She looked at Grandma, and at that moment Grandma happened to close one eye in a wink. Maggie was only five but that wink told her plenty.

"I wanna stay with Grandma," she said.

"I guess that settles it," said Grandma.

"Well, we'll see," said Aunt Ruby. She wasn't convinced but for the time being she withdrew.

Grandma and Maggie got along very well. Grandma went to work every day in a restaurant where she cooked hamburgers and made sandwiches. On the way to work she left Maggie in a day-care center, and picked her up on the way home. They cooked supper, washed the dishes, and then sat together watching television or telling stories. The stories were mostly about the time when Grandma was young, and lived with her cousins in a beautiful big house. She had two girl cousins, Esther and Bertha, and a boyfriend named Hank. They all rode bicycles to school, and Hank teased them. Maggie loved to hear about that time.

"Tell about the cousins," she would say. And Grandma told what they did, and described their house. It had a porch all around, and a big attic, and a beautiful garden with white iron seats and flowers in a ring of seashells, and ducks swimming in a pond.

"Some day let's go there," Maggie would say.

But Grandma never heard from her cousins any more. Esther, the one who still lived there, used to send Christmas cards. But none had come in a long time. So Maggie thought of the cousins' house as something in a story.

When she got older, and could go to school and come home alone, she would go to the store, take the wash to the Laundromat, and put the potatoes on to boil before Grandma came home. Grandma said she was a great help and had lots of sense.

"It's lucky I have you, Maggie," she sometimes said. "I need somebody to keep me in order."

Maggie agreed. Living with Grandma was full of surprises. That wouldn't have mattered except that Aunt Ruby still hadn't given up. She was forever popping in, complaining that Maggie didn't eat the right things, never went to bed on time, and had unsuitable playmates. She said the street where they lived was getting worse all the time and they should move. There had been burglaries. Stores and houses had been broken into.

Grandma said, "I have been here twenty-five years and I'm not moving now."

It was true that the apartment houses were shabby, with cracked front steps and broken windows, their walls decorated with smears of paint and words that Aunt Ruby probably didn't even know the meaning of. At night there were weird noises—screams and shouts and raucous laughter. But Grandma wasn't worried.

She said, "It's just kids. I've seen plenty of them. They'll grow up and get married and you'll never know they were once a bunch of wild animals."

Aunt Ruby looked out of the window at the teenagers wearing strange caps and T-shirts and shuddered.

"We've got friends here," Maggie assured her.

Maggie's best friend, Diane Ramon, was eleven and a half. Their birthdays were two days apart. Diane's father was the super. Her mother and Grandma were friends. Grandma told Mrs. Ramon where to get bargains, how to fill out her tax forms, and how to cure a cold. (Hot tea with lemon and whiskey was good for nearly everything.)

Then there were Maggie's other friends in the apartment house. Marcus lived with his uncle and often didn't get enough to eat when the uncle spent all his money on wine, or didn't go to work. Pedro lived with his mother and stepfather and a crowd of little brothers and sisters. Laurie was younger but tagged after Maggie like a little sister.

The five of them played out in the street when the weather was good, or, in winter or bad weather, mostly in Maggie's house.

Marcus liked to draw with Magic Markers. He covered paper bags and wrapping paper and even newspaper with wild colors.

Pedro was smart in school and liked to read. But at home he had little chance, with all the children yelling and the television blasting away.

Laurie loved cats, and was always bringing home some hungry stray, which her mother promptly threw out.

Diane and Maggie were always building houses. It was their favorite thing.

"Some day my papa's gonna take us to the country," Diane said. "When we came from Puerto Rico he said he was gonna save up a lot of money and get us a house."

"Me and Grandma will go too," said Maggie. "We'll have a big house like her cousin Esther's, with room for everybody."

Then they would pile up boxes, and make furniture out of odds and ends. Now they were making a real dollhouse in Maggie's room. It took up a lot of the floor. Mr. Ramon gave them wood and showed them how to use a hammer and saw. Maggie was getting good with tools and was thinking of being a carpenter some day.

But what about today?

Suddenly Grandma banged her cup down on the table.

"If we're going, let's get started," she ordered. "Get the kids while I pack the food."

Maggie ran to alert her friends. Soon they were ready. Diane had a flight bag containing her Thermos bottle, a sweater and a cake that her mother had baked.

Pedro had a book and a bag of grapes. Laurie had a box of Oreos. Marcus had nothing.

"My uncle didn't buy anything," he said miserably. "Maybe I better not go."

"Don't be a dope," Maggie told him. "We have plenty."

They started walking toward the river, Grandma going at a leisurely pace and the kids running ahead, playing tag, hiding behind parked cars and jumping out at each other.

At Riverside Drive they waited for a bus.

Suddenly Grandma said, "Oh, shoot!" and stuck her arm out to hail a cab.

"Grandma!" said Maggie. "What are you doing? The bus is coming."

"So is Christmas," said Grandma. "The cab is more fun."

The cab pulled up and the kids piled in back. Grandma got in front with the driver.

"Take us to the picnic grounds across the bridge," she said.

Maggie shook her head disapprovingly. Sometimes Grandma got out of hand. Still it was fun to ride so luxuriously.

The cab sped along the drive and then on to the bridge, high over the water. The view of the great river was breathtaking. The children stared out of the windows.

"Hey! Look at that big ship! Look at the sailboats! Look at the cliffs!"

Grandma leaned back and smiled as if she had arranged the scenery for their benefit. The taxi driver glanced at her now and then as if he was wondering if she had enough money for the fare but didn't dare ask. At last they were across the bridge. Grandma paid him with a royal gesture as if she took taxis every day. Then they hiked off along the shore to the picnic grounds.

Pedro made the fire and soon the hot dogs were roasting on a rack over the flames. A few minutes more, and everyone was feasting on potato salad, hot dogs and rolls, tomatoes, pickles, cake, cookies and fruit.

When they were so stuffed that they had no more room, Grandma brought out the box of marshmallows.

"These don't take up any space," she said.

Dreamily they toasted marshmallows and licked the foamy sweetness off their fingers.

"That was good," sighed Marcus. "I wish I could eat like that every day."

"Look at my stomach," said Diane. "I got fat."

8

"You kids can work off some of that by playing ball," said Grandma. "I'm taking a nap."

Maggie, Diane, Laurie and Marcus started for the ball field, where some boys seemed to be in need of extra players. Pedro stayed behind and opened his book.

"What's wrong with you?" Maggie asked. And Grandma said, "Did you just come here to read? Don't you want to play?"

Pedro looked embarrassed. "I don't wanna be a drip," he said. "But, see, at home I can't study. They told me if I do this extra work I can get into high school a year early. So I brought this along. Is it okay?"

"You do whatever you want," said Grandma. "Come up to our house if you want. I never was much for studying myself, but I wouldn't want to discourage you."

And she leaned back on the pile of sweaters and closed her eyes.

At last the afternoon began to wane. The sun was far over in the west. It was time to go home. They gathered up their things.

"This time we'll take the bus," said Maggie. "We're not millionaires." Grandma did not protest.

They rode back across the bridge, staring at the ribbons of lights twinkling along the highway, and the patterns of the lighted windows in the high buildings. At last they were walking along their street and up their own front steps.

"That was pretty sneaky of you, Grandma, taking a cab," Maggie said as they climbed to the top floor. "Who do you think you are, Mrs. Rockefeller?"

Grandma grinned. "Hate to wait for buses. Stupid

things. You wait half an hour and then six of them come at once. Seems like they only travel in herds."

"But the money, Grandma!"

"Well, they say you can't take it with you. And you can't say it wasn't fun!"

"Yes, it was great," Maggie said. "The kids liked it too. Come on, we're almost there."

"Good. I'm getting hungry. Have we anything in the house to eat?"

"No. I didn't go shopping," said Maggie. "Nothing but tuna fish and spaghetti."

"Well, that will have to do."

They arrived at the top floor and Grandma was reaching for her key, when she stopped and gasped.

A light shone under their door.

"Somebody's in there!"

"Don't, Grandma," said Maggie. "Don't open the door. It might be a burglar. I'll call Mr. Ramon."

"Nobody's going to break into my house without asking me," said Grandma. And she put her key in the lock.

"Grandma!" Maggie screamed. "Don't! They might have a gun!"

Grandma swung her pocketbook, ready to hit, when the door opened.

"Well, it's about time," said a voice.

It was Aunt Ruby. Maggie and Grandma stood speechless.

Aunt Ruby was the first to speak. "Where have you been? I've been waiting all day and nothing to eat but some canned spaghetti and tuna fish."

"Ruby!" said Grandma. "How did you get in?"

"The super's wife let me in," said Aunt Ruby. "And what a time I had convincing her! I had to threaten her."

"But why didn't you let us know you were coming?"

"I wanted to phone you but you have no phone. Well, come in, don't stand there."

"I'll come in if you'll stand out of the way," said Grandma, with dignity.

Aunt Ruby stood aside and Grandma walked past her and sat on the couch with a thump. She closed her eyes and leaned back.

"Grandma, are you all right?" Maggie asked.

"Just a little tired," Grandma said. "The shock, seeing Ruby there. I thought—a burglar—"

"Would you like your sherry?" Maggie asked anxiously.

"Yes, that will pick me up," said Grandma. "Get some for your aunt too."

"Never touch it," said Aunt Ruby, through tight lips. "And as for your being tired, Susan, that's what I came to talk to you about."

"Some other time," said Grandma. "Ruby, sit down, you make me nervous."

Aunt Ruby stood tall and stiff and scowling.

"I must talk to you now," she said. "I've been waiting all day."

"Yes, and what do you mean by sitting in my house when I'm not here?"

"I had to tell you something," said Aunt Ruby. "I'm getting married."

"Oh! Congratulations! Who is the lucky man?"

"He is a doctor. We are leaving for California in a week, and I intend to take Margaret Agnes with me."

Aunt Ruby was the only person who called Maggie by her full name. She hated it.

"I won't go!" she exclaimed.

"Maggie," said Grandma, "get the sherry. Then we'll hear what your aunt has to say. Now calm down, Ruby, and take a seat."

"I *am* calm," said Aunt Ruby. "And I have no more time. Morris is waiting to take me to dinner. I just want to tell you we are leaving a week from today, and we will take Margaret Agnes with us. She can come for a visit so she will see how nice it is there. I am sure she will want to stay."

"I won't," said Maggie, coming back with the sherry and a glass of Coca-Cola on a tray. She held out the Coke to Aunt Ruby.

"Terrible stuff," said Aunt Ruby. "Morris says it is dangerous to the lining of the stomach. Never mind. I don't want anything. Margaret Agnes, you be ready. You won't need to pack much. We'll buy you clothes in California. Something besides those awful pants and shirts. And you'll look better with your hair trimmed."

Maggie was proud of her long brown hair and thought it looked nice. She looked at her grandmother. Why didn't she say something? But Grandma seemed to have no opinion. She peered up over her sherry glass.

"It's up to Maggie," she said. "I think I'll go and lie down. Ruby, you'll have to excuse me. This has all been too much for me." And she walked slowly toward the bedroom, as if she was too tired to talk any more.

Maggie was not fooled. Left alone with Aunt Ruby, she decided to face up to her.

"I'm sorry, Aunt Ruby," she said, "I can't go with you. I like it here. I've got lots of friends and I like my school. And besides, Grandma needs me."

That turned out to be the wrong thing to say. Aunt Ruby looked more determined than ever.

"This is the most important time of your life," she said. "You're almost twelve. We must think about your future, send you to a good school, where you'll associate with a good class of children, not like those little ragamuffins you play with. Why, we don't even know what your talents are."

"Yes, we do," said Maggie. "I'm going to be a carpenter and build houses. Mr. Ramon is teaching me."

"Ridiculous," said Aunt Ruby. "And as for your grandmother needing you, it isn't right for a young girl to spend her time taking care of an old woman. I can see how old your grandmother is getting. Old and feeble. She won't be able to work much longer. Then what will you live on?"

"I guess she'll get a pension," said Maggie. "And of course I can work."

"Well, don't worry. You won't have to. We'll take care of her. There are homes where old people can be looked after. I have made inquiries. I'll tell you all about it on the plane. Good-bye."

And with that she walked out, slamming the door.

Maggie, in a rage, gave it a kick.

_____TWO

"Well, what else did your aunt have to say?" Grandma asked, emerging from the bedroom.

"She's got it all planned," Maggie said furiously. "I'm supposed to go with her and go to a good school so I don't have to spend my most important years taking care of you. And you're to go to one of those homes for old ladies. Ugh! I hate her! Aunt Rhubarb! I'm so mad I could scream."

"Now, Maggie," Grandma said. "She has a point. I'm not getting any younger. What if I got sick and you had to take care of me?"

"She said you're getting old and feeble and should stop working," Maggie said.

Grandma grinned. "I did sort of lay it on thick," she

said. "I was hoping she'd leave. I didn't want to ask her to supper. Speaking of supper, let's get busy. You said there was tuna and spaghetti."

"There was, but she ate them."

"What a nerve! Sitting here and waiting like a spider, and eating our food! Who let her in, anyhow?"

"Mrs. Ramon, she said."

Just then there was a knock at the door.

"I hope she hasn't come back," said Grandma. "Go put the chain on the door and if it's her, slam the door."

But when Maggie peered out she saw the anxious faces of Diane and Mrs. Ramon.

"We brought you this," Diane said.

"We afraid you don't got supper," said her mother. "That lady, she eat up everything and talk, talk, talk. Here, you take this."

She held out a large, steaming pizza. It smelled wonderful.

"Oh, Mrs. Ramon, how kind of you!" said Grandma. "How did you know?"

"She make me let her in," said Mrs. Ramon. "I tell her nobody home but she say she's Maggie's aunt. She sit on stairs if I don't open the door. She say this terrible house, not fit to live in. I get mad, give her piece of mind. I want to call police, but my husband, he say she can make trouble. Maybe she report him. He afraid to lose his job. So excuse him, please."

"That's all right," said Grandma. "You couldn't help it."

"I feel bad. And you so nice to Diane and all the kids. So I bring the pizza."

"Well, thanks. You saved our lives. We were just

going to starve to death. Come on, sit down. Maggie, make some coffee."

Maggie put the kettle on. She poured coffee for Grandma and Mrs. Ramon, and some orange drink for herself and Diane.

"Gee, that was a great day we had, Mrs. Miklusky," Diane said.

"Well, we'll do it again soon," said Grandma. "My, this is good pizza, Mrs. Ramon. Did you make it?"

"Sure I make. You think I buy from that no-good guy on the corner? Eat, you need your strength."

"What do you mean?"

"That lady makes trouble for you."

"Oh, come on," Grandma laughed. "How can she do that?"

"She come down, use my phone, because you don't got phone. Call up an old-age home. I hear her. She say she need place for old lady. Who that means?"

"I guess that means you, Grandma," said Maggie.

"Nonsense," said Grandma. "Eat that pizza before it gets cold. Diane, you have some too. We'll talk about Aunt Ruby tomorrow."

Mrs. Ramon went downstairs, but Diane stayed and helped demolish the pizza. Then the two girls washed the dishes.

Diane remarked, "Mama didn't like that lady. Even if she is your aunt."

Maggie said, "Who could like her? She wants to take me to California."

"You're not going!"

"No, of course not."

"But can she make you go?"

"I'd like to see her try. Mean old witch, I hate her."

"But why was she phoning that old-age home?"

"She's got an idea in her head that Grandma's getting too old to work. Then after we got home, Grandma put on this act as if she was weak and tired, just to get rid of her. I guess that convinced her she was right. Aunt Rhubarb, I call her."

Diane picked up the pizza plate. "I better go now. We had fun today, didn't we? Your grandma is a real good sport. Maybe tomorrow I'll come up and we'll work on our house."

Maggie and Grandma were left alone. Grandma said, "Well, is there anything good on TV? Or shall we have a game of Scrabble?"

"But what about Aunt Rhubarb?"

Grandma chuckled. "We got rid of her all right."

"But she may come back."

"We'll think of something," said Grandma. "Go on, set up the board."

Sunday it rained.

"Good thing we had our picnic yesterday," Grandma said. "Today we can take it easy. Do the crossword puzzle. How about pancakes for breakfast?"

She dumped flour, eggs, and milk into a bowl and splashed in sugar lavishly. Soon the pancakes were sizzling in the pan, golden brown and bubbly. As they were sitting down, there was a timid knock at the door. Maggie opened it.

There was Marcus. His shirt was crumpled as if he

had slept in it, and his hair stood out in several directions.

"What happened?" Maggie asked.

"My uncle," said Marcus. "He didn't come home. It's three nights now."

"Why didn't you tell us?"

"I didn't want to spoil the picnic."

"Well, sit down and have breakfast and we'll think what to do."

While Maggie set another place and Grandma made more pancakes, Marcus said nothing. He just looked worried and glum. When they sat down to eat, he devoured the first four cakes.

"You can stay here today," Grandma said. "He's stayed out before."

"I can't eat your food all the time," said Marcus. "One time he stayed away three weeks."

"Maybe we should call the police," Grandma said. "He has no right not to take care of you."

"No!" Marcus exclaimed. His face wrinkled with fear.

"Why not?"

"If you call the cops, they'll start to look for him. They might put him in jail."

"He deserves it," said Grandma, flipping another pancake onto his plate.

"Yes, Grandma," said Maggie, "but don't you see, they'll take Marcus away someplace. They did it before."

"Why?"

"He's a kid, so they say he can't stay by himself. They'll put him in some foster home."

"Is that bad?"

Marcus said, "No, but first they put you in the shelter."

"What's that like? Are they mean to you?"

"Some of the big kids are real mean. And it's so boring. There's nothing to do." He sat with his head down, looking at his fingers. "I could run away," he suggested.

"That's right," said Grandma. "Show some spirit. But you'd need money. Can't run away without money."

"No," Marcus sighed. "And then the teacher would say why wasn't I in school."

Maggie said, "Why can't he stay here? He could go to school and they'd never know. Anyhow there's only one more week of school."

"Of course," said Grandma.

"But then I'd be eating your food," said Marcus.

"We could make you work. Then you'd earn your keep till your uncle gets back. What can you do, Marcus?"

"I can draw," said Marcus. "You want something drawed on?"

"I know," Maggie said. "He could paint the kitchen. Mr. Ramon is too busy. He has two jobs."

"Good idea," said Grandma. "We'll see about getting paint."

"Okay," said Marcus, brightening up and starting to eat again. "Gee, these pancakes are good."

"Go get your clothes," Maggie ordered after breakfast. Marcus ran down to get his things. He brought them up in a laundry bag.

"He can put them in the bottom drawer," Grandma said.

"No, he can't," said Maggie. "They smell. He'll have to wash them. Take them to the Laundromat, Marcus. Wait, I'll go with you and be sure you don't put too much soap in."

"Might as well take ours too while you're at it," Grandma suggested.

Maggie went and came back, leaving Marcus to watch the clothes.

Grandma was sipping another cup of coffee and reading the Sunday paper. "My, the things that go on," she said. "Look at this. You remember last week some crooks broke into a big jewelry store downtown?"

"What about it?" Maggie was not interested in jewelry stores. "Did the cops catch them?"

"No, but some woman was out walking her dog and she found a box with some rings in it, on the street. The cops say it's from that store. She found it in our neighborhood, just a few blocks away!"

"You mean they dropped some of the loot a week later, uptown? Pretty stupid burglars."

She nibbled a cold pancake and started putting the dishes in the sink, when there was a soft knock at the door.

"Now what?" said Grandma.

It was Laurie. She was all wet, and she was crying. In her arms she held a small, scrawny black cat. Her tears dripped into its fur. It struggled to get loose.

"Mama says I have to throw it out," she wailed. "And it's raining. What'll I do?"

"Come in, you're all wet," Maggie said. "Why are you so wet?"

"I was sitting on the stoop. Then I saw Marcus and he said I should come here."

"Get a towel and dry her," said Grandma. "This seems to be trouble day." Maggie dried off Laurie and the cat. The cat escaped and hid behind the refrigerator.

"Here, have a pancake," said Grandma. "And give the cat some milk. Then you'll both feel better. Why doesn't your mother like cats? Is she allergic?"

"No, I don't think so," said Laurie, sniffing. "She just doesn't. Maybe I could take the kitty and run away, but I don't know where to run."

Maggie felt sorry for Laurie, sitting on the floor watching the kitten lap milk with its tiny red tongue. It seemed too bad that she should not have her own pet kitten to play with.

"Grandma," she said, "maybe we could keep the kitten here for a few days. Then Laurie could come and visit it."

Grandma considered. "Well, if it won't make a mess."

"Oh, no, she's a good kitty," said Laurie. "I had her in my room for two days and she had a box to go to. I fixed it for her with newspaper, and she always went. But Mama found her."

"Well, all right," said Grandma. "We'll see how it works out."

Laurie jumped into her lap and hugged her.

Just then Marcus came back with the load of wash. He was excited.

"Did you hear?" he said. "Some guys broke into the TV store and robbed it last night!"

"The TV store! You mean on our street?" said Maggie.

"Yep. They cut the glass and got in and took out all the TV sets. The store is a mess. The man is there now with the cops. They're roping off the street."

Maggie said, "But that's the store Mr. Ramon works in."

"Poor Mr. Ramon," said Grandma. "He has luck, but it's bad."

"Why is he poor?" Marcus wanted to know. In his view, anybody who had a family and three meals a day was rich.

Grandma explained. "He has two jobs. He is trying to save up enough money to have his own store so he doesn't have to be a super. He'd like to have a house too, in the country. The Ramons came from a farm and don't like the city. Now he'll lose a few weeks' work, I guess, till the store gets going again."

There was another knock at the door.

"Now what?" said Grandma.

"It was Pedro, scowling and looking very angry.

"What's with *you*?" Grandma asked.

"Could I leave my books here?" Pedro asked. "My stepfather says he'll tear them up. He wants me to go to work and not be studying all the time. I'd run away, only Mom would feel bad."

"Everybody is running away, it seems," said Grandma. "Maggie, is there anything we have to run away from?"

"There's Aunt Rhubarb," Maggie said.

"Oh, well, I wouldn't run from her," Grandma said. "I wouldn't give her the satisfaction. Now, Pedro, you go in the living room and study, and the rest of you go in Maggie's room and keep quiet, and I'm going to my room and take a nap."

Quiet reigned. The rain rained too, thumping on the roof with a cheerful, busy sound. It lulled Grandma to sleep and soothed Pedro's troubled mind.

In Maggie's room, Maggie, Marcus and Laurie worked on the dollhouse. Maggie was making furniture out of spools, little boxes and bits of cardboard. Marcus decorated the walls with his Magic Markers. Laurie cut out paper dolls from a magazine. After a while Diane came to join them. She brought pieces of cloth to use for bedspreads and rugs. But her mind wasn't on the dollhouse.

She was upset because the cops were asking her father all kinds of questions, as if he were a crook and had helped to rob the TV store. Her mother was crying and it was all terrible.

But after a while she cheered up and got to work. Laurie put the kitten inside the dollhouse, and it knocked everything over trying to escape. The radio played softly.

At last it began to get dark, and Maggie switched on the lights. Pedro came in looking dazed from studying, his hair sticking out in all directions.

"What time is it?" he demanded. "Six o'clock? I'll get killed. I better go. Gee, I got a lot of work done. Thanks. So long."

Grandma sat down in her rocking chair.

"Almost time for supper," she said, yawning. "Maggie, you'll have to go down to the deli. Get some cold cuts and two cans of baked beans and—"

Diane said, "Wait, don't go yet. I think my mother made a lot of chili. I'll go and see."

In a few minutes she was back with a big bowl. "Mama says they're going over to see my aunt and don't need this. And she says I can stay."

So Grandma, Maggie, Diane, Laurie and Marcus and the kitten sat down to eat chili, washed down with cups of tea. Afterward Marcus was sent down to buy ice cream.

"It'll be nice having Marcus," Grandma remarked. "He doesn't mind running errands."

"I wish I could live here too," said Laurie, cuddling her kitten.

Grandma laughed. "Where would I put so many people? Go see if there is something nice on TV."

So they all sat and watched "All in the Family." It was a rerun they had seen before but they enjoyed it.

"It feels like a family," Marcus said.

Grandma answered, "Well, if this is a family and I'm the head of it, then I say we better go to bed. Laurie, you go on home. The kitten will be all right here. Marcus, you sleep in the living room. I have to go to work in the morning even if I am old and feeble. Ha!"

_____THREE

Monday morning came, and Maggie, Marcus and Grandma had to get up and get ready to go out.

"Only one more week of school," Maggie said.

"And what am I going to do then?" Marcus muttered.

"Oh, your uncle will be back by then," said Grandma. "Put on a clean shirt. That one is too dirty. And brush your hair and teeth. I'll feed the kitten. Better shut her in Maggie's room. No, she'll knock over the dollhouse. Put her in my room. Good-bye now."

"Wait, Grandma!" Maggie cried. "What if you get home first and Aunt Ruby comes and I'm not here?"

"Don't you worry. I can handle her," said Grandma loftily. "I wasn't born yesterday."

But Maggie was doubtful. "Don't promise her anything. And don't put on one of your acts. Good-bye."

She walked down the stairs, frowning uneasily.

"What's the matter?" Marcus asked.

"Oh, I don't know," said Maggie. "Grandma might do something silly, just to get Aunt Ruby's goat. That old witch just needs some excuse to grab me away."

"What does she want to do that for?"

"She thinks Grandma should be in an old-age home and I should go to California and have my hair cut and wear dresses."

"Maybe we better all run away," said Marcus.

School that day was mostly fun and games, but Maggie couldn't enjoy it. Grandma had said not to worry, but she did worry. However, when she got home all was peaceful. Grandma had come home from work and was preparing to fry chicken.

"That boy needs feeding up," she said. "It's a shame the way he's been neglected. And look at that little cat. She's drunk half a pint of milk."

The kitten was curled up on a cushion, a round little ball with a fat stomach that puffed up and down as it breathed.

A little later Laurie came to play with the kitten, and Pedro came to do homework. It was a happy family scene. It seemed as if all was right with the world, when the doorbell rang and Diane burst in, followed by her mother.

"Oh, Mrs. Miklusky!" exclaimed Diane. "Maggie! We just heard from the super next door. They caught two of the guys that robbed the TV store. Hey Marcus, what do you think? One of them is your uncle!"

Marcus turned pale. Grandma said, "Now look what you did. Scared the boy out of his wits. What happened?"

Mrs. Ramon said, "They catch him trying to sell TV on 125th Street. Put him in jail. But the main guy got away."

"What am I gonna do?" Marcus said in a weak voice.

"Do? Nothing. You'll stay here, as we decided."

"But they'll come and get me," he said. "It happened before."

"Nonsense," said Grandma.

"He is right," said Mrs. Ramon. "They say his uncle not a good guardian. They put him in a foster home."

Maggie spoke up. "Why can't this be his foster home? Grandma can be his foster mother."

"Foster grandmother, you mean," said Grandma. "Very well, that's what we'll tell them if they ask."

But Marcus shook his head. "They won't let you. They have to ask a bunch of questions and find out if you can take care of me and have an extra room and if you're home all day."

"That means you can't go to work, Grandma," said Maggie.

"Oh, well, maybe I'll retire," said Grandma.

At this moment there was a loud sputtering from the stove and the kitchen was filled with smoke.

"Now look, the chicken burned!" Grandma scolded. "Everybody get out of here and calm down. Nothing is going to happen."

She put the chicken in another pan. "I guess a little charcoal won't hurt us. It's time for my sherry. And the kids can have grape juice. Marcus, stop worrying."

"I got to go now," said Mrs. Ramon. "The mister, he got to go to the store, answer a bunch of questions. They drive him up the ceiling."

"Up the wall, Mom," said Diane.

"Ceiling is higher than the wall," said her mother.

The children sipped their juice and Grandma went back to her cooking. Soon chicken, rice and tomatoes were on the table and they were about to sit down when there was a loud knock.

"Who is it?" Grandma demanded.

"Is Laurie there?" an angry voice replied. It was Laurie's mother. She stood there, a large woman with brassy blonde hair.

"I don't think so," said Maggie. "I don't see her. She was here playing with the kitten but she left."

Laurie's mother said angrily, "That kid spends so much time here, maybe you should adopt her *and* the cat."

Grandma said, "She's a nice little girl. She's just crazy about cats. I can't see that that's a crime. She wants something to love. Come on in and have some chicken. Move over, kids."

"No, I can't stay," said Laurie's mother. "I've got somebody waiting for me to go out. I just wanted to give her her supper. She must be playing with some other cat someplace. Can't stand cats. They give me the creeps. But that Laurie, I can't get it through her head. Maybe you'd like to keep her. I'll pay you."

"Don't know as I can take in another kid," Grandma said, smiling. "But I'll think about it and let you know."

"I mean it. You can have her. And if you see her, tell

her she's going to get it when she does come home."
And she walked out slamming the door.

"Can we eat now?" Grandma asked. "It's getting cold."

They had barely sat down and picked up their forks, when a little voice said "Hi!" It was Laurie, covered with dust, with the kitten in her arms. The kitten struggled and protested. But Laurie clutched it tightly.

"Where were you?" Maggie demanded.

"Under the bed," said Laurie.

"You bad girl. Your mother was so upset," said Grandma.

"No, she wasn't upset," said Laurie. "She said I could stay with you and she'd pay. Can I, please?"

"Nonsense," said Grandma. "Sit down and eat."

"Not till she washes her hands and face," said Maggie.

"Well, make it fast," said Grandma. "And I hope that's all the excitement for one evening."

But it was not. At about eight o'clock, when the dishes were done and the TV switched on, Diane and Mrs. Ramon reappeared. Maggie looked at their faces, trying to decide whether they had further news to deliver, or whether this was just a friendly visit.

"Sit down, Mrs. Ramon," Grandma said. "You remind me of the fellow on the news, always coming up with the latest horror story. What now? Nothing has happened for at least an hour. Have they caught the mad bomber or has something been hijacked?"

"You always laughing," complained Mrs. Ramon. "Is not funny. Too bad you no got phone. Then I no have to climb stairs."

"Come on, Mrs. Ramon, you didn't need to come. You could send Diane. You know you like to come to see me. What is it now?"

"Is Maggie's auntie phone," said Mrs. Ramon. "She phone just now. Say she coming tomorrow with doctor. Want you to meet him."

"Tomorrow!" said Maggie. "I thought she wasn't coming back till next week!"

"She must have changed her plans," Grandma said.

"I'll stay home from school," Maggie said.

"Indeed you won't," Grandma declared. "She might decide to kidnap you. Leave it to me. I'll handle her."

Mrs. Ramon was right, Maggie thought, walking to school the next morning. Grandma didn't take Aunt Ruby seriously enough. She acted as if it was all a joke.

It was lucky that nothing important was going on in school, for Maggie could not have kept her mind on her work. All the problems at home kept churning in her mind. Marcus, Laurie, Pedro, the Ramons, Grandma. What if Aunt Rhubarb really could somehow get her away? Who would be there with a little common sense? Grandma was so reckless. She didn't care what she said.

Maggie hurried home from school, hardly listening to Laurie babbling about her kitty, or Marcus gloomily wishing his uncle would get lost altogether. Even Diane was looking blue.

"What's wrong with *you*?" Maggie asked her.

"The TV store," Diane said. "You know my papa works there part-time. Well, the man said they cleaned him out and he's gonna close the store. So Papa will lose his job there. We were gonna take a trip. Papa got an old car and fixed it up, and we were gonna go to the mountains and camp out. Now I guess he'll have to sell the car."

Maggie sighed. Everybody had trouble. They went into the building, Diane to her apartment on the ground floor and the others up the stairs to the top. Laurie rushed ahead, in a hurry to see her kitten. She had decided on a name for it—Coalie, because it was as black as a piece of coal—and wanted to see how the kitten liked it. But Maggie dragged her feet.

However, as they got close to the top floor, the sound of voices reached her—voices raised in argument, coming from her apartment. The door was closed but the noise was very audible. Maggie went in.

There was Grandma, standing in the kitchen doorway, brandishing a big iron frying pan. Facing her were Aunt Ruby and a man who Maggie thought must be the doctor her aunt was going to marry. He was tall and thin and sour looking, like Aunt Ruby herself. *Dr*. Rhubarb, Maggie thought. They turned as the children entered.

"Oh, Margaret Agnes," said Aunt Ruby. "I'm glad you are here. Maybe you can get your grandmother to listen to us. She's upset."

Aunt Ruby's normally pale face was red. Grandma, however, did not look particularly upset. She just stood there with a little smile on her lips, waving the pan back and forth.

"Yes, do come in," she said. "This is Dr. Bean. I have

just told him that if he doesn't leave my house I'll bean him with this pan."

Aunt Ruby said, "Dr. Bean is a noted authority on aging. He knows all about what's best for old people. I want him to examine your grandmother, but she is not cooperating. Now tell these children to go home so we can have a talk." She glared at Marcus and Laurie.

"I can't, Aunt Ruby," said Maggie.

"Why not?"

"They *are* home. They live here."

"Live here! What do you mean by that?"

"They are foster children," said Maggie. "They live here with us."

"I certainly didn't know that," said Aunt Ruby. "They will have to be sent somewhere else."

Maggie felt it would be better not to argue about Marcus and Laurie at the moment. She told them to go into her bedroom and shut the door. Then she said, "Why should he examine Grandma? She's not sick."

"No, but she is getting quite old and feeble, and we are concerned about you. Dr. Bean knows of a very good old-age home where she will be very happy, but she can't get in unless she acts reasonably."

"And what if she doesn't?"

"Then I fear there are other places," said Dr. Bean.

Aunt Ruby must have thought this was going too far, for she suggested, "Now why don't we sit down and have a calm discussion?"

Maggie was anxious for them to leave. If they didn't, she knew, Grandma would do something outrageous and that would only make matters worse.

"Grandma," she said, "didn't you go to work today?"

"No," said Grandma. "I felt dizzy and then I saw some little green men trying to get in the window. I decided I better stay home and watch them."

"Grandma!" Maggie shrieked.

Grandma put her hand to her head and said, "This excitement has been too much for me. There they come again. Dr. Bean, they're after you!"

Maggie said, "Grandma, you go and lie down."

"Will you watch them, Maggie? All right, I'll go." And she staggered out of the room.

Maggie offered to make some tea.

"No, never mind," said Aunt Ruby. "But you see how it is, Margaret Agnes. We mustn't let her get upset. We'd better go now, but we'll come back tomorrow."

Dr. Bean said, "Keep her as quiet as possible. Light food, and no exertion, and don't let her climb the stairs. They are bad for her. And try to convince her that a change would do her good. She'll listen to you."

They left. But a minute later Aunt Ruby was back. "You must get rid of those children," she said. "I'll contact a social worker to take care of them. Good-bye."

At last she was gone. Maggie sighed with relief. But only for a moment. The children came out, very upset.

Marcus said, "She's going to send me to the shelter. I know it. I'll run away."

Laurie said, "I'll have to go back to Mama, and leave Coalie." And she began to cry.

"Now stop that, all of you!" Grandma ordered, coming out of the bedroom.

"Are you all right?" Maggie asked.

"Of course I am," said Grandma. "I only pretended to be crazy to get rid of them."

"But they'll come back."

Grandma leaned close to Maggie and said, with a wicked wink, "What if we're not here when they come back?"

"Then they'll keep coming."

"But she said she was getting married and moving to California. Sooner or later they'll have to go. So if we can just keep it up long enough—"

"Go out every day," said Maggie.

"What about school?" Grandma asked.

"It's almost over."

"We could go on a trip."

"But where? And what about your job?"

"I'll take my vacation time."

Marcus and Laurie looked from one to the other. Then Laurie asked, "Are you going to let those bad people get us?"

Maggie said, "We'd only go away for a week or so, till Aunt Rhubarb goes to California."

"But who will we stay with?" Marcus asked. "They'll take me to the shelter."

"And Mama will throw out Coalie," said Laurie, getting ready to cry. "I want to go with you."

"We can't take you along," said Maggie.

"Why not?"

"Well, we don't even know where we're going," Maggie said. She watched Grandma walking up and down the living room. Suddenly she had an idea. "Grandma! I just thought where we can go."

"Oh, good! Where?"

"To Cousin Esther's house."

"Cousin Esther! But I haven't heard from her in ages."

"Maybe she'll be glad to see us," said Maggie, "that is, if she's still there."

"I never heard that she moved—or died," said Grandma. "But we don't know if she wants company. I don't even know if she can afford to have us."

"Well, she has that big house," said Maggie. "She must be rich. We'll just drop in on her. Aunt Ruby will never find us."

"It's not a bad idea," said Grandma, slowly becoming convinced. "She hasn't seen you since you were little. I think we owe it to her."

"What about us?" Laurie asked again.

"Oh! Yes, well, I suppose we could take them along. But we'd have to ask Laurie's mother."

"What about your job, Grandma?"

"I've already asked for leave. That's why I came home early today. Now, Maggie, you go down and speak to Mrs. What's-her-name. Tell her we're going to the country for a week and is it all right if we take Laurie along. And bring her clothes."

"Goody!" said Laurie, jumping up and down. The kitten's head and tail bobbed up and down as she jumped.

Maggie went down, and soon returned. "She's not there. We'll have to talk to her later."

There was quiet for a while. Maggie couldn't help thinking about something Marcus said: maybe we should all run away.

35

"Where does Cousin Esther live?" she asked.

"Where? Oh, in a village," said Grandma. "It's called Mountainside."

"But where is it? How far? How do you get there?"

"It's upstate. We take a bus, I imagine."

Marcus had been sitting quietly, saying nothing. Now he asked, "Can you drive?"

They stared at him. "Drive? We haven't got a car."

"Mr. Ramon has," said Marcus.

"We can't take his car," Maggie said.

"You heard Diane say they can't go away because the TV store was closing. They might have to sell the car."

"It's a fine idea," said Grandma. "I could rent it from Mr. Ramon. Of course. It will be our get-away car!"

Maggie could see she loved the idea.

"But can you drive, Grandma?"

"Don't insult me, girl," said Grandma. "Of course I can drive. Haven't done it in some time but it will all come back. I'll go and speak to Mr. Ramon right now."

In a little while she was back in high spirits. Mr. Ramon was not averse to renting her his car. He was worried about getting a parking ticket and this would get it off the street for a while. After that he would see. With all his troubles he didn't need parking tickets.

"Come, now, we have to pack," said Grandma. "We must be out of here the first thing tomorrow morning, before those people come back. No doubt this time they'll bring a nurse and a wheelchair for me. Let's see, it's summer, so we don't need too many things. Still, up in the mountains it may be cold."

"Does she live in the mountains?"

"Well, yes. There are mountains all around," said

Grandma. "Bring sweaters, all of you. And extra jeans, and bathing suits."

"I don't got no bathing suit," said Marcus, "and only one pair of pants."

"How can I get my stuff if Mama doesn't come home?" Laurie asked.

"You can't even go till we get her permission," said Maggie.

"But what about my kitty?" Laurie wailed.

"Don't worry, we'll take care of her."

"We can't just leave the child here," Grandma said.

"You can't take somebody's kid," Maggie declared. "It's kidnapping. She could have us arrested."

"No, she said she'd pay us to take care of her."

"But we didn't say we were going away."

"Who's going away?" a voice asked. It was Pedro.

"Oh, you scared me. It's a secret," Maggie said. "Close the door. And swear not to tell."

As Pedro listened in amazement she filled him in. He exploded.

"Put Grandma in a home!" he yelled. "She's got more brains than everybody else put together. I'll kill them!"

He was so angry that his face got red and his fists clenched. He was ready to punch Aunt Ruby and her doctor in the nose if they dared to show up.

"Don't worry," Grandma said. "We'll be away before they come back. The main thing is, they mustn't know where we are going or they may follow us. But what I'm worried about now is clothes. Marcus hasn't enough, and Laurie's are in her apartment and her mother's gone."

Pedro looked at the children and said, "Maybe I can

dig up some things for them. Some of our kids are about their size."

He went off, and Maggie and Grandma went on packing. Canned foods, bread, crackers, cereal, plastic dishes went into boxes.

Maggie had to go to the store for more food—fruit, tomatoes, bologna and hot dogs and rolls for cookouts, and cheese, milk and cookies. "We'll save money that way," Grandma said. "Restaurants are expensive."

"Money!" said Maggie. "Do we have enough money?"

"It's too late to go to the bank," said Grandma. "There's the money in the teapot." (This was where Grandma put her odd change.) "And I have my paycheck. Here, take it to the store, and see if they'll cash it. When we get to Esther's, no doubt she'll lend me some money."

"We need a flashlight," Maggie said.

"My uncle has one," said Marcus. "I'll go and look."

By the time Maggie had returned from the store, Marcus was there with a flashlight, some blankets, and a few tools: a screwdriver, a hammer and a small saw. "I thought they might come in handy," he said.

"That's a good flashlight," said Pedro, who had just come in with an armload of clothes.

"My uncle uses it in his work," said Marcus.

"How'd you get all those clothes?" Maggie asked Pedro.

"I said I was going to the Laundromat with them. They need washing. I'll take them down and wash them, then they'll be clean."

"Now I mustn't forget one important thing," said

Grandma. "Mr. Ramon has to show me how to work the car."

That sounded ominous to Maggie, though the others didn't notice.

"Can we all go?" they asked.

"Better not. A crowd would be too noticeable." She went off to find Mr. Ramon while Maggie went on packing. Pedro brought back the clean clothes. There were some jeans and sweaters that were just right for Laurie, and some pants and shirts for Marcus.

"What if your mother asks where those things are?" Maggie asked.

"We've got so many kids, she can't keep track," said Pedro. "Gee, I wish I was going along."

"I wish you were too," said Maggie. "But we have two extra kids already. I don't know what Cousin Esther will say. Of course, she's probably rich, so it won't matter."

She looked at his downcast face and couldn't stand it. "Hey, Pedro," she said, "you know what? As soon as we get there tomorrow, I'll see what the place is like, and maybe you could come up on the bus. I mean if there's lots of room and Cousin Esther is glad to see us and all."

"Hey, that's a good idea," said Pedro. "Okay, don't forget."

FOUR

It was six o'clock in the morning. The house was quiet as Grandma, Maggie, Laurie and Marcus got ready to creep down the stairs, carrying blankets, boxes, coats, shopping bags. Laurie had her kitten in a covered box. The kitten was scratching and struggling to get out. It didn't care for this mode of travel at all.

"Now remember, Laurie," Grandma told her, "we'll ring your mother's bell and ask her if you can go. If she says yes, okay. If not, no. And no crying, understand?"

"Okay," said Laurie, unhappily.

But when Maggie opened the apartment door, something white lay on the floor outside. It was an envelope. Maggie put down the box she was carrying and picked it up.

"It's for you, Grandma," she said.

"It's from Laurie's mother," Grandma said.

> Dear Mrs. Miklusky,
> I had to go away on a short trip. Please take care of Laurie till I get back. Thanks a lot.

"Well, that solves your problem, Laurie."

"Hooray!" Laurie yelled.

"Keep quiet. We don't want the whole street to know."

Mr. Ramon was waiting for them. "Come on," he said. "I show you where is car. I don't bring her here because somebody might see."

Lugging their possessions, they stole out into the street. The air was fresh and cool. In the east, the sky was pink with the sunrise. Only a few people were out—a couple leaning unsteadily on each other after an all-night party, a man hurrying toward the subway, a skinny cat scratching in a trash can.

"Oh, look!" cried Laurie. "The kitty is hungry!"

"Come on," Maggie whispered. "We're not taking any more cats."

Around the corner was the car, a big black old station wagon with one crumpled fender.

"There she is!" exclaimed Grandma. "Our get-away car."

"I get her from my friend in filling station," Mr. Ramon said. "Some guys leave her there. Say they come back, never show up. He fix her up. She run pretty good. Now, Mrs. Miklusky, you remember how she go?"

"I think so," said Grandma, climbing into the driver's

seat while the others stowed themselves and their belongings in the rest of the car. "Let's see, I turn the key, step on the gas, and away we go."

"No, no! That's not first," Mr. Ramon squawked. "You kill everybody. Be careful. Is my car. If you have accident I go to jail."

Grandma winked at Maggie. "Just having fun with him," she said. "Okay, I'll be careful. Now remember, Mr. Ramon, if anybody asks, you don't know where we are. I'll phone you when we get there."

"Don't know nothing!" he promised. "But don't forget to phone."

"Now have we forgotten anything?"

"Yes!" said Maggie. "The radio and the teapot. I'll go back."

They all waited impatiently while Maggie ran back upstairs.

"Radio is good idea," said Mr. Ramon, "but why you need teapot?"

"That's where I keep my money," said Grandma. "Here she is. I don't know what I'd do without that girl."

Maggie, gasping for breath and clutching a portable radio and a teapot full of nickels, dimes and quarters, sank into the seat beside Grandma. They were about to pull away, when there was a loud shriek. "Wait! Wait!"

Diane and her mother came running. Mrs. Ramon was clutching a pot. "I make you some chili," she said.

"And here are some tacos," said Diane.

"Thanks a million," said Grandma. Marcus stowed the food in the back among the blankets.

"I wish you were going too," Maggie said. "Maybe when we get there, if it's all right, you can come."

"Yes, we'll drive out. Oh, no, we can't drive, you have the car."

"Maybe we'll come and get you, if Aunt Ruby goes to California with her boyfriend. Meantime you can work on the dollhouse."

"I couldn't, without you," Diane said, shaking her head sadly.

Now Grandma did turn the key. The motor roared.

"Not so hard!" Mr. Ramon yelled. "She old! Take it easy!"

"I'm old too," said Grandma. "Don't yell at me." And off they went.

They moved through the nearly empty streets. Grandma's driving was a little jerky.

"Where's the signal thing?" she muttered, turning a corner. "Oh, here it is!"

"Hey, Grandma, you're on an east-bound street. You can't go west."

"Well, I want to go over to the river," said Grandma. "Too late now. We'll have to keep going." Fortunately no other cars were moving. Coming to the river, she turned north. Mists were rising.

Marcus said in amazement, "I never was out so early before!"

"Me either," said Laurie, opening the kitten's box a little. "Look, Coalie, want to see the river?"

But the kitten was not interested in scenery. She just wanted to get out of the box. She squeezed out and hopped on the back of Grandma's seat.

"Get that cat off my neck!" said Grandma, slamming on the brake.

Laurie put the kitten back in the box. "How's that pot of chili?" Maggie asked. Marcus reached over and poked at the blankets.

"Hey!" he yelled.

Grandma stamped on the brake, causing them all to pitch forward in their seats.

"What's the matter?"

"I touched something soft," said Marcus. "Something alive!"

Grandma pulled over to the curb. As they turned to look, the blankets rose up in a hump and separated, and a head appeared.

"I came too," said Pedro, grinning foolishly.

"You stowed away!" said Maggie. "What's the idea?"

Pedro stopped grinning. "I couldn't stand it," he said. "That guy is always after me to go to work. I passed the test, I could get in the special school but he won't let me. I said I'd run away and I will. If you don't want me, I'll get out here. I have money. I can get along. I'll get a job."

He sat angrily among the blankets, looking so ridiculous with his red face and tangled hair that they all laughed.

Then Grandma said, "Well, you've come this far, you may as well go along. It's only for a few days. But won't they be worried?"

"No," said Pedro. "I left a note. I said I heard about a job for the rest of the summer upstate and I'm going to see about it. I'm fourteen. I can work."

"Okay," said Grandma, "let's get going. We're headed upstate too."

"Where to?" Pedro asked.

"I'm not sure. I thought we'd ask as we went along."

"Grandma!" Maggie yelled, horrified. "You don't know where we're going?"

"I told you, Mountainside," said Grandma. "Stop worrying. I'll know it when I see it."

There was a wicked twinkle in her eyes but Maggie was too worried to notice. "Do we have a map?" she asked.

"Well, no, we were in such a hurry. I thought I'd get one when we stop for gas. Now calm down. I know we go up the Hudson and over a bridge. Now everybody keep still. I have to pay attention to my driving."

It wasn't long before they came to a tollbooth. Grandma reached into the teapot, dumped a handful of nickels into the basket, and they shot forward onto the parkway. The old car sped along as if it was glad to be out of the city.

"She certainly rides well," said Grandma. "Makes a fine get-away car. I wonder who owned her."

Maggie said, "We'll probably never know. Well, it doesn't matter. She does go fast, doesn't she?"

"Yes, indeed." Grandma was enjoying herself. Her white hair blew back in the breeze. She began to sing softly, "Sailing, sailing, over the bounding main—"

Suddenly Maggie noticed a sign: Speed Limit 55.

She peered at the speedometer. The needle seemed to be pointing at 65, then 70, then 80. "Grandma," she yelled. "Slow down!"

"Oh, yes," said Grandma. "Don't want to get Mr. Ramon in trouble."

They were out in the country now. Trees along the parkway were covered with white and pink flowers. Birds sailed in the sky.

"It's nice out here," said Marcus. "But where are the people?"

"What people?"

"Don't any people live here?"

"Sure," said Maggie. "The houses are back among the trees."

Laurie said, "I bet you could have lots of cats out here."

"Cats!" said Pedro, disgustedly. "Don't you ever think of anything but cats?"

"Yes," said Laurie. "I'm thinking something else right now."

"What is it?"

"I'm hungry."

That reminded them they were all hungry. They had been up since five o'clock, and had eaten a very skimpy breakfast.

The car's clock said eleven. "Let's stop and eat, Grandma," said Maggie. "It's eleven o'clock."

"It can't be that late," said Grandma, looking at her watch. "It's only eight thirty. The clock isn't working. It's too early to stop. Besides, the signs say No Picnicking." The truth was, she was enjoying herself too much to stop. But she agreed that they would look for a suitable place. Several miles further on, a sign said Service Station.

"Should we get gas, Grandma?" Maggie asked.

"No, the tank is three-quarters full," Grandma said. "Let's wait. Gas is probably cheaper off the parkway."

But a little further along, Maggie said, "Grandma, I think we better stop and eat. Everybody is hungry."

"No place to stop here," Grandma said. "I'll pull off at the next exit."

As she turned into a side road, the car began to sputter strangely. It seemed about to stall, but Grandma managed to coast to the shoulder of the road and stop.

Maggie took out the picnic box and they sat down in the grass. Soon they were stuffing themselves with rolls, cheese, bananas, cereal and milk.

"Do we get chili too?" Pedro asked. "I been smelling that chili ever since we started."

"No. That's for lunch."

"This is the best meal I've had since—since yesterday," Marcus said, patting his stomach. "Soon I'll be getting fat."

And indeed he did look better than the skinny waif he had been a week ago.

"We'll have to get you some bigger clothes," said Grandma. "All right, now, let's get going. I want to get there before dark."

They hurried back to the car with the remains of their breakfast. But when Grandma attempted to get going, the starter whirred but the motor would not catch.

"What's wrong? Why won't she go? She was going fine a few minutes ago."

"No," said Pedro. "You remember, she stalled just before we got here. Maybe she's out of gas."

"But the gas gauge said she was three-quarters full."

Maggie said, "But that's what it was when we started. I remember looking. I guess the gas gauge is like the clock. It doesn't work either."

"She must be empty," said Pedro. "I'll walk back to that service station and get a can of gas." And he started off.

"Wait! Pedro!" Grandma called. "Take some money." She handed him a five-dollar bill.

Pedro hurried away. Half an hour later he was back, lugging a heavy can. He unscrewed the cap and poured the gasoline into the tank.

"That's fine," said Grandma, starting the motor. "Where's the change?"

"He kept the whole five," Pedro said. "It's a deposit on the can."

"What a robber!" said Grandma. "Well, get in, and let's go."

She swung back onto the parkway and headed north.

"Grandma!" said Pedro. "Aren't you going back to return the can? The man owes you money for it. And we need more gas."

"No," Grandma said. "I can't stop to look for the southbound entrance. We'll take the can with us. We'll fill up at the next place."

"But we need a map," said Maggie.

"And I have to go to the bathroom," said Laurie.

Ten miles further on they stopped at another filling station.

"Fill 'er up," Grandma ordered. "You kids go to the bathroom. And Pedro, go in the office and get a map of New York State. And you, young man, clean off the windshield and check the oil and water." She sat back, watching the man work.

The children came back and they started off again. This time Maggie and Pedro squeezed into the front seat and spread out the map they had found.

"This here road is what?" Pedro asked.

"The Taconic Parkway," said Grandma.

"And where does your cousin live?"

"Mountainside. It's a small village."

"I can't see it. The car jiggles too much."

"Well, I can't stop now. Can you see a bridge on the map?"

"Yes, here's one, near Poughkeepsie."

"That's not the one we take. Where's the next one?"

"Looks like Hudson."

"That's the one."

They zoomed along smoothly, except for an occasional clank from the back of the car.

"What's that?" Maggie asked.

"Oh, nothing," said Grandma. "The car is going, isn't it?"

"I just wondered. Let's see if the radio works. No, it doesn't. Well, good thing we brought our own."

She lifted the small radio from the floor and pushed a button. Their ears were assaulted with a blast of rock music.

"Turn that off!" Grandma ordered. "Or find something better."

"Why, Grandma, that's nice music," said Maggie. "You're out of date." But she fiddled with a knob and was rewarded with a weather report: "Today promises to be seasonably warm, partly cloudy with a chance of scattered thundershowers."

"Looks like we missed the news," Maggie said. "Well, who cares? Here's some music." This time a folksinger rendered "Oh, Susanna."

"That's what I call singing," Grandma said, and they all joined in with "Oh, Susanna, oh don't you cry for me, for I'm off to Louisiana with my banjo on my knee." Then they had "I've Been Workin' on the Railroad," and then "Home on the Range."

"That was pretty good," said Grandma, "but it's made me a little bit sleepy. Think I'll take a nap."

"Not here, Grandma," said Maggie.

"My goodness, girl, don't you think I have any sense? I mean when we come to a stopping place."

They went on until a sign announced: Scenic Overlook. Grandma pulled in and stopped the car in front of a low stone wall.

"Feast your eyes on the scenery, children, while I take a rest. I declare, I'd forgotten that driving a car was work." And she leaned back and closed her eyes.

The children climbed out and looked around. They were on a high bluff. Below them was a green valley planted with fruit trees in neat rows, and beyond that were hills. Still further off were mountains, rows and rows of huge humps, fading off into the blue distance.

"Gee!" Marcus whispered. "I never saw anything like that!"

None of them had. They all stood and stared at the view, forgetting everything else, until Maggie said, "Hey! What's that?"

Something soft and woolly had bumped her from behind, like a big sofa cushion. It was a dog with thick woolly hair that hung down over its face. It stuck its cold wet nose into her hand.

"Who are you?" she asked. The dog wagged its tail. She looked around to see who owned it. There was nobody in sight except a young man with a pack on his back. "Is it yours?" she asked.

"I guess so," he said. "I was hiking along and she came and joined me. I think she's lost, so she adopted me."

"Oh, she's a girl," said Maggie.

The dog had now transferred her attention to Marcus. She put her paws on his shoulders and licked his face. Marcus put his arms around her. "She likes me," he said.

"Hey, Marcus, don't get too friendly with her," Maggie warned. "She might want to go with us."

"It's a bad place for a dog," said the young man. "She might get hit by a car."

"I wonder where she came from," said Maggie. "She must have jumped out of somebody's car."

"She has no collar on," said the young man. "I thought I'd take her with me till I find a policeman."

Pedro had been investigating the underside of the car. Now he came out covered with dirt. "I was trying to see what made that clanking noise," he said. "The exhaust pipe is loose."

"Pedro!" said Maggie, impressed. "How did you know that?"

"I read a book about cars," he said. "I look at them too. I could fix it if I had some wire."

The young man rummaged in his backpack and

pulled out a ball of cord. "Will this do till you get a wire?" he asked.

The next minute, both of them were stretched out on their backs under the car.

"What's going on there?" Grandma asked, waking up.

"We fixed the car," said Pedro. "Something was loose."

"I knew we'd be glad we took that boy," said Grandma. "But who is this?"

"My name is Peter Paul Halloran third, ma'am," said the man. "I'm on my way home from college. Stopped to admire the view."

"Oh! Where's your car?"

"No car, ma'am. Hitchhiking. You wouldn't be going across the river?"

"Yes, we are," said Grandma. "Can you drive?"

"Yes, of course," said Peter Paul Halloran third.

"I'm a little tired of driving," said Grandma. "I wouldn't mind having somebody take a turn. Get in."

"Grandma," said Maggie, "we have to look at the map."

"Oh, yes." They spread out the map and bent their heads over it. "Here's what we do," Grandma pointed out. "Take the Hudson–Catskill bridge. Mountainside isn't on this map. It's too small. But it's beyond Middleburg, near Cobleskill. It's way up there. See, you turn off the main road and take Route 145. Well, let's get going."

"But is there room for the dog too?" Peter Paul asked. "I can't leave her here." Grandma agreed she could be squeezed in. The kitten, however, felt differently. Faced with this monster, she fuzzed up her tail and spat.

"Help!" Laurie yelled.

"Put the cat back in the box," Maggie ordered. "The dog won't hurt her. It's just till we find someone to take care of her."

"*I'll* take care of her," said Marcus, hoisting the dog into the back of the wagon and climbing in after her.

At last they were off again. Peter Paul drove very well: not as fast as Grandma, but much straighter, Maggie thought. He went slowly over the bridge, so they could look down at the river flowing calmly along. Here and there on its surface were some little boats, a slow-moving barge, and a big white ship with flags flying.

"That's some river!" said Marcus.

"Yes, one of our best," said Grandma, as if it was all her doing.

They crossed the bridge and were soon rolling along a country road.

"Isn't this pretty?" said Grandma.

"Yes, it's nice," said Maggie, noticing a marker, "only it isn't 145, it's 23A."

"Oh," said Peter Paul. "I turned left there. I should have turned right."

"Well, it doesn't matter," said Grandma. "Pull off under that big tree and we'll look at the map again. Looks like rain, doesn't it? Maggie, turn on the radio and see if there's a weather report."

Peter Paul pulled over and unfolded the map while Maggie turned on the radio. A voice said, "Police are looking for a black station wagon with license number 303-NM2."

"Hey, we've got a black station wagon!" Maggie cried.

"Yes, but it's not 303-NM2," Pedro said. "It's 70-PKF."

"How do you know?" Maggie asked doubtfully.

"I looked," he said.

She wasn't satisfied, however, and got out to check. Sure enough it was 70-PKF.

"Well, that's good," she said. "I thought Aunt Ruby was on our trail already."

"She couldn't be," said Grandma. "How would she know, unless Mr. Ramon told her. So don't worry. This isn't the only black station wagon in the United States."

Peter Paul wanted to know who Aunt Ruby was. When they told him, he nodded. "I've got one like that, only it's an uncle. He's expecting me home any minute now. I'm supposed to go to work in his office and learn to be a lawyer."

"Won't you be—er—a little late, taking a detour like this?" Grandma asked.

Peter Paul grinned. "I don't mind," he said. "Let's say I'm not in a hurry to be a lawyer."

"What do you want to be?" Maggie asked.

"I'm not quite sure," said Peter Paul.

FIVE

The sky darkened and soon the rain came down. It was past lunchtime but it was raining too hard to have a picnic. Pedro suggested that they could just sit in the car and eat chili.

"But it's cold," Maggie said.

"Chili is good whatever way you eat it," said Pedro.

So Maggie got out the pot of chili and spooned it into plastic bowls.

Then they drove on until they came to a diner at a crossroads. It was called The Blue Moon.

"I wonder why they call it that," said Maggie.

Grandma said, "Maybe people only eat there once in a blue moon. Let's go in and see. I need a cup of coffee."

They ran through the rain, leaving the kitten and the dog to guard the car, and seated themselves on stools at the counter.

The diner was not a very inviting place. It was grubby, the counter top had spots on it, and the woman behind it was a drab-looking person with stringy hair and a droopy gray sweater. She looked at them as if she was surprised to see them there.

The fly-specked menu listed hamburgers, hot dogs, and cheese sandwiches.

"I'll have a western," said Grandma.

"What's a western?" the woman wanted to know.

"You don't know? I'll make it myself. Have you got onions, peppers and eggs?"

And she marched behind the counter, broke some eggs onto the steel plate, stirred them with onions and peppers, and slapped them between two slices of bread. The woman stood watching her, astonished.

"That looks good, Grandma," said Maggie. "Make me one."

Soon everybody was asking for westerns.

"I don't want to use up all the eggs," said Grandma, "Mrs. er—"

"Grombecker," said the woman. "Don't worry, we have more eggs than you can shake a stick at. We have all those chickens."

"Where?" Peter Paul asked.

"Out there on the farm," said Mrs. Grombecker.

"You have a farm?"

"Yes. We have three hundred chickens and six cows and we can't get any help. My husband wants to sell, but nobody will buy it. I'm running this diner to make a living but folks say they don't like my cooking. I've tried everything. Waffles, pancakes—"

"Why don't you make westerns?" Maggie asked. "You'd get rid of the eggs."

"Well, I don't know how. Maybe I could if she would show me."

"And how about some fresh coffee?" Grandma asked. "I'd like some."

Mrs. Grombecker filled an old battered coffeepot with water and put it on the stove. "I've got an urn but it broke."

"Well, you better get it fixed. With all those cows you must have plenty of cream. People want a good cup of coffee."

"You couldn't give it away free," said Mrs. Grombecker. "Folks just don't come in here any more."

Pedro had found the coffee urn on a table in one of the booths and begun fiddling with it.

"You got a broken wire," he announced. "I could fix it. Then you could give the coffee away free. Hey, Marcus! Get that screwdriver you brought."

"That's a smart boy," said Grandma. "He's right. A big sign outside: Free Coffee With Your Westerns. And for goodness sake clean the place up. Now we have to be going."

"Oh, no, don't go yet," said Mrs. Grombecker. "It's pouring. You better show me again how how you made that—uh—western."

"All right," said Grandma. "You take a couple of eggs, beat them up, add the onion and pepper, and by the way, you can serve them on toast, rolls, anything they want. Now where is everybody? Maggie, go find Laurie and Peter Paul. Marcus, what are you doing?"

Marcus had found a big cardboard poster advertising last year's movies. He turned it over and with his Magic Marker made a sign:

A FREE CUP OF COFFEE

WITH YOUR WESTERN

FRESH EGGS AND CREAM

FROM OUR CHICKENS AND COWS

"Is it all right?" he asked.

"It's very nice," said Mrs. Grombecker. "But I don't know, I'll have to ask my husband—"

"Could I have another western?" Marcus asked.

"Yes, take this one," said Grandma, giving him the one she had just made. Marcus put the sign in the window and ran outside to see how it looked.

"Now, come on, Maggie, I thought you were rounding them up."

Maggie reported, "Marcus is feeding his western to the dog. Laurie is crying. She took her kitten to the barn and it ran away and got mixed up with a lot of other kittens and they are all hiding in the hay. And Peter Paul is helping milk the cows."

"I fixed the coffee thing," Pedro announced. "Now let's plug it in and see if it works." He poured a potful of water into the urn and switched it on. They waited for it to blow a fuse but it didn't.

"Now can we go?" said Grandma.

But just then a car pulled in and a man and woman got out. They hurried inside, rainwater dripping off their hats.

"We'll have a couple of those westerns and that free cuppa coffee you advertised."

"Advertised?" said Mrs. Grombecker.

"Well, you have a sign in the window," said the man. "Is it for real?"

"Oh! Oh, of course," said Mrs. Grombecker. But she whispered to Grandma, "You'll have to do it. I haven't learned how yet."

So Grandma whipped up a couple more westerns and poured coffee out of the old pot, as the urn was not boiling yet.

Meanwhile a woman and two children walked in.

"We thought the rain had stopped so we went for a walk," she said. "We're staying at the hotel and the children are so bored. But then it started to pour. I'd like one of those westerns and coffee. But what have you got for kids?"

"Well, there's cookies and milk," said Mrs. Grombecker.

Grandma opened the refrigerator and looked in. "I tell you what," she said. "You need some supplies. I'll make a list and you go to the store while I mind the diner."

She grabbed a pad and started to write: doughnuts, candy bars, ice cream, chocolate syrup, bacon, tomatoes, bread, butter, sliced cheese, cupcakes, chopped meat, cold cuts, ketchup, rolls.

Mrs. Grombecker looked doubtfully at the list. "Isn't that an awful lot?" she asked. "It'll be a lot of money."

"Charge it," said Grandma. "You'll soon have lots of trade or I miss my guess. And hurry back."

As soon as she had left, Grandma seized a rag and some soap and washed off the counter. "Maggie!" she ordered. "Go out and pick some flowers. Weeds will do. Pedro, one of those stools is wobbly. See if you can fix it. I feel sorry for that woman, I don't know why. She's so helpless."

By the time Mrs. Grombecker came back the diner looked like a different place. Each table had a glass of water with a few flowers in it. Marcus had decorated the menus with the words *Free Coffee*. The storm had passed and now over in the west the sun shone on the dripping trees.

Peter Paul came back from the barn, and reported that Laurie was still looking for her kitten.

Grandma sat down in one of the booths and wiped her face with a napkin.

"I wouldn't mind a cup of coffee," she said.

Peter Paul brought her one, and sat down to have one himself. He had a happy smile on his face. It was a peaceful scene. But Maggie felt she had to interrupt it.

"Grandma," she said, "it's getting late. Shouldn't we go?"

"Yes, as soon as we can catch Laurie."

"Where are you staying?" Mrs. Grombecker asked.

"We're on our way to visit my grandma's cousin," said Maggie. "But we won't make it if we don't start now."

"Is she expecting you?"

"Not exactly," said Maggie. "But we wanted to get there. If we don't we'll have to stay in a motel."

"And we can't afford a motel for all those kids," Grandma added.

"You can stay here with us. We have room. Please. We owe it to you. Look what you did for us."

Grandma considered it. "Well, if you're sure there is room."

"There are three empty bedrooms in the farmhouse. And you can show me more about those sandwiches. Oh, here's my husband. Mike, this lady helped me this afternoon."

Heavy steps were heard and a big, bearded man walked in. He carried a pail of eggs in one hand and a small radio in the other.

"Evening, all," he said. "Brought some eggs. Just getting a weather report." He set the radio down and they all listened while a man told about low-pressure systems and scattered thundershowers.

"And now," he went on, "for the latest news." He then told about a grange meeting, a car crash, somebody's cow getting out and trampling Mrs. Somebody Else's garden, and a lost dog.

Nobody was much interested in the news until the voice said, "Parkway police are still looking for a black station wagon with the license number 303-NM2. A black wagon was seen on the Taconic when it stopped for gas. A woman was driving, but the man was busy and did not notice the number. At another service station a boy gave a deposit for a can of gas but did not return the can. Parkway police have been cruising but have not seen the car."

There was silence after that, broken by the sound of the dog whining and barking from the car.

Peter Paul said, "I guess she needs to go for a walk. She's been in that car a long time."

"I'll take her," said Marcus.

Mr. Grombecker watched him. "Hey!" he said, "isn't that a black wagon you got out there?"

"Where?" said Grandma, starting up in alarm. "Oh, that's mine. You had me worried for a second. It's all right. That's not my number. Must be looking for somebody else."

Marcus was walking the dog along the road. The farmer watched him. "What kind of a dog is that?" he asked.

"Don't know, some kind of mixture," said Grandma. "We haven't had her very long."

"Thought I heard something on the radio about a lost dog," said the farmer. "Funny you having a black wagon *and* a dog."

"Oh, stop fussing," said his wife. "This lady has been helping me all afternoon. Can't you see how nice the place looks? She showed me how to make westerns and the boy fixed the urn that I've been after you to fix for a month, and the other boy made the sign."

"What sign? Free coffee! Are you crazy, woman?"

"It's to bring in the customers," said his wife. "We've had six already. And it uses up the eggs."

"I have it!" said Maggie, suddenly. "I've been thinking and thinking and now I know what to call the diner. The Great Western!"

The farmer shook his head doubtfully. He was against it.

"We'll talk about it later," his wife said. "Now come

on, I'll show you the rooms." She led the way to the farmhouse, got out some sheets, and opened the bedroom doors. "Now you lay down and have a rest," she told Grandma. "You must be tired. I'll fix supper. Maybe this girl can help me. What did you say your name was? Maggie?"

"I'll go down in a few minutes," Maggie said. "First I want to help make the beds."

"Oh, that's right. Get 'em done before dark. Then you can turn in early. I wish I had a smart girl like you." And she hurried out.

Maggie closed the door after her. "That Mr. Grombecker thinks it's us the cops are after," she said. "Maybe we ought to go."

Grandma nodded and beckoned to the boys. "Come here, I don't want to talk too loud. Maggie is right. He suspects us. I can't understand it, though. If Ruby is on our trail and knows we have a black wagon, why do they keep giving the wrong number?"

"She must have found out from Mr. Ramon," Pedro surmised. "Maybe she tortured him, the way they do in war movies. Then maybe he gave her the wrong number to throw her off the track."

"That could be it," said Grandma. "But in any case, we have to be out of here tomorrow at the crack of dawn. If we aren't, I bet that farmer will call the police. We must tell Peter Paul. By the way, where is Peter Paul?"

"He's helping Mr. Grombecker feed the chickens," Marcus said. "Where is Lucky gonna sleep?"

"Who is Lucky?"

"Our dog. I decided to call her Lucky."

"Oh. Well, she can sleep in the car. Go on, now make your bed."

Dinner was a silent meal. The farmer sat at the head of the table and ate as if it was a job he had to finish. The children ate plenty, too. In spite of their egg sandwiches, they were hungry, and they consumed several packages of Mrs. Grombecker's cupcakes and ice cream. Peter Paul kept falling asleep.

"Guess I'm not used to farm work," he said apologetically after his head had nearly fallen in his plate three times.

Laurie was not happy. Her kitten refused to be found. She dripped tears into her ice cream.

After supper, Maggie helped Mrs. Grombecker with the dishes, while Mr. Grombecker, Grandma and the boys watched TV and Laurie sniffed sadly. Maggie nervously peeked into the living room now and then, hoping there wouldn't be another news broadcast, but the show was just an old western film.

"Seems to be our western day," she thought. In fact, Marcus was now working on a new sign saying:

THE GREAT WESTERN DINER
GOOD EATS
FRESH EGGS

When the movie was over, Grandma herded the kids out of the living room.

"Get your pajamas and toothbrushes out of the car, and make it fast," she ordered.

"Can't I look for Coalie one more time?" Laurie asked.

"We'll let Coalie sleep in the barn tonight, with the other cats," Maggie said. "Tomorrow morning we'll find her. And tonight you can sleep with me so you won't be lonesome."

Marcus was afraid Lucky would be lonesome in the car, but Peter Paul said he would sleep there with her.

_____SIX

The sky was barely light when Grandma and the children crept quietly down the stairs and out to the car. Lucky greeted them happily, leaping about and whining with joy as if she had not seen them for weeks.

"Be quiet," Marcus said. "We don't want to wake everybody up."

"And please stop crying," Maggie said to Laurie. "We'll find you another."

Laurie's kitten was not to be found. They had gone to the barn and searched the hayloft. If the kitten was there, it took care not to be seen. They had to come down, covered with bits of hay, trying to comfort Laurie.

"I hate to go away without saying good-bye to Mrs. Grombecker," said Grandma, "but I think it's good if we get an early start. I left a note for her on my pillow. Where's Peter Paul?"

Peter Paul and his backpack were both missing. In their place in the car was a note.

> Dear folks:
>   I found out what I want to do. Instead of working in a law office I'm staying on the farm. You can keep Lucky. Thanks for the lift.
>
> Au revoir,
Peter Paul

"What's *au revoir*?" Pedro asked.

"It means till we meet again."

"Oh, like *hasta la vista*. That's nice."

"Very nice," said Grandma. "Especially the dog. One more thing to take care of."

"I'll take care of her," Marcus said, putting his arms around her. Lucky stuck out a long red tongue and washed his face. Then both of them settled themselves in the back of the car.

Grandma turned the key. With a loud roar the motor started.

"I'm going to miss Peter Paul," Grandma remarked.

"But we have Lucky," said Marcus.

"She can't drive," said Grandma.

It was a little eerie driving in the gray light of early morning. The children were still sleepy and did not talk much. The trees overhung the road, like big ghosts in patches of fog. The road seemed to be going uphill.

"We better stop for a look at the map pretty soon," Maggie said. "And have breakfast. That will cheer Laurie up."

"And me," said Grandma. "I need my coffee. Maybe we shouldn't have left in such a hurry. We could have had coffee."

"There's a little chili left," Pedro suggested.

"Ugh! Cold chili for breakfast! You do have some weird ideas. We'll stop at a diner and get breakfast. We're bound to come to a village soon."

But they drove on and on, passing farms where cows were walking slowly out of the barns, or a man on a tractor was cruising across a field.

To take their minds off their empty stomachs, Maggie turned on the radio. It was dead. Its batteries were burned out.

"I guess we don't get any more news till we can buy some new ones," she said.

"What do we need news for?" Pedro answered. "We can see what the weather is like, and if they want to look for black cars, let them."

The sun came up, the mists cleared away, and still no village appeared. All around were hills.

"It's beautiful," Maggie breathed. "If only I weren't so hungry. Look, we have bread and cheese. Let's eat that. And there's a barn with a gas pump in front of it. Maybe they'll give us some water to drink."

"Hey, Grandma," Pedro said, "maybe we better get gas. Our gauge isn't working, remember? We could get stuck again."

Grandma nodded and pulled up to the gas pump. But there was a sign on it: Not Working.

Not far away was a house, and on a tree there was another sign: For Sale.

"I'll ask at the house," said Maggie. "Maybe they'll give us some water."

She went to the door and knocked. A young woman came out. Her hair was tied up in a large blue kerchief. She wore ragged jeans, cut off short, and a man's shirt, and she looked harried.

"What is it?" she asked. "Do you want gas? We're not selling gas now. Sorry."

"We saw the sign," Maggie said. "We just wanted some water. And could we eat a picnic in front of your house? We haven't had breakfast yet."

"Haven't had breakfast!"

"No. We started early and got lost and couldn't find a diner. Grandma thought we could stop and eat and look at our maps."

"Would your grandma like a cup of coffee?" the woman asked. "I have some left over."

"Oh! That would be wonderful," said Maggie. "That will fix her up."

"Here, take the pot. It's still hot. And what about some milk for the kids? I see you have several. Go on, take it. I would only throw it away."

"Throw it away!" Maggie couldn't believe it.

"Yes, we're leaving tomorrow. Or the next day."

Maggie took the coffeepot and the bottle of milk, and filled her Thermos with water for the animals. They sat under a big tree near the road and ate bread and butter, cheese and fruit. Grandma felt much better after the coffee.

"This is a fine place," she said, "right on top of a hill

with a view of all those mountains and valleys. I wouldn't mind staying awhile."

"Grandma!" said Maggie. "You know we have to get to Cousin Esther's."

"Oh, yes. I forgot. What on earth are those people doing?"

The young woman and a young man, also in torn-off jeans, were hauling things out of the house. They hoisted a rolled-up rug and laid it on the grass. Then they brought out a trunk and a table.

"They must be moving," said Pedro. "That's what we did when we moved. Put everything outside."

But then the young people carried out a box of glass-ware and arranged the things on the table.

"That's not moving," said Grandma. "They're having a yard sale."

"What's that?" Maggie asked.

"It's what you have in the country when you want to get rid of things."

"Let's go help them," Maggie said.

Marcus jumped up and Lucky jumped with him.

"No, don't take Lucky. Leave her in the car."

They packed up their things and went to the house.

"Thank you for the coffee," Grandma said. "I might have murdered somebody if I didn't get some. I see you're having a sale."

"Yes, we're moving," said the young woman. "Tom, bring out another table for the china."

"You'll have to give me a hand," said Tom. "This one's heavy."

"We'll help," said Pedro. "I'm strong." He rushed into the house and heaved up one end of the table.

"I'll put the china out if you want, Mrs. um—"

"Allen. Mary Ann Allen. And that's Tom."

"Too bad to move," said Grandma. "You've got a lovely view."

"You can't eat a view," said Tom, scowling.

He lugged a couple of chairs down the steps. Pedro went and got some more.

"My grandfather left me this place," said Mary Ann. "The farmers used to come here for gas, and Grandpa had a repair shop and fixed their cars and tractors for them. And Grandma was a nurse and took care of anybody that was sick. But I'm no nurse. I make pottery, and Tom—well, he knows about cars but he can't get anybody to help him, and anyway he's more interested in making furniture. So we're going back to the city."

Grandma examined the glass and china spread out on the table.

"That's some pretty nice stuff you have there," she said. "And those chairs are real old, aren't they? My mother had some like them. You ought to make plenty selling them."

"I don't know," said Mary Ann. "The people around here haven't got a lot of money to spend, and we're pretty far off the main roads where the tourists go. I did advertise in the local papers and on the radio. A few people have looked at the house. Oh, Tom, you best put the sign up."

Tom went to the barn and got out a big sign saying:

YARD SALE

EVERYTHING MUST GO

REASONABLE

He leaned it against the big tree.

Grandma shook her head. "I don't like to butt in," she said, "but could I offer a few words of advice?"

"Of course," said Mary Ann, "but I don't think it will do much good."

"First of all," said Grandma, "don't say 'Reasonable.' Say 'Fantastic antiques.' And don't say 'Everything must go.' Say 'While they last.' Pedro, go get Marcus. Marcus, get busy and make another sign. Now, let's see, what kind of prices have you got on those things? Oh, my, they're too low!"

Mary Ann said, "But the farmers around here can't afford high prices."

"No," said Grandma. "You need to attract the tourists. Let's change some of those prices."

She grabbed a pencil and started doubling the prices that Mary Ann had put on the things.

"But that's too much!" Mary Ann protested.

"They're worth a lot more," said Grandma.

"Grandma, how do you know?" Maggie whispered.

"There was a lady used to come into the restaurant. She had an antique shop. She had a bunch of old washboards and flatirons, just the kind my mother used, and she wanted ten bucks apiece for them. These are real nice things. Now don't put any more out till you see what happens."

"Grandma," said Maggie, pulling her sleeve, "we have to go."

"Oh, yes," said Grandma. "Stop worrying, Maggie. I declare, you're a regular old woman. I forgot what I was going to say. Oh, yes, it's going to be hot today. You could make some lemonade. People like that. And take that sign off the gas pump. Some folks will need gas. That is if you have gas in there."

"Sure we do," said Tom. "But I have no time to pump it."

"I'll do it," said Pedro. "I know how. I can fix cars too."

"Pedro is a real smart boy," said Grandma. "Come on, I'll help you with the lemonade. We could whip up some brownies. That'll get them."

"Grandma," said Laurie. "Can I sell the lemonade? I always wanted to sell lemonade."

"Of course. Marcus can make another sign. Lemonade ten cents a glass. Homemade brownies. We better hurry. It's past eight o'clock. That is," she said to Mary Ann, "if you want me to. I almost forgot it's your kitchen."

"I'd be delighted," said Mary Ann, "but I don't know why you should do this."

Before Grandma could say "Because it'll be fun" or "I just feel like it," Maggie interrupted.

"Well, you gave us the coffee and the milk," she explained. "And we do need gas."

Tom said, "Gas? Just drive up to the pump and I'll fill her up."

While Grandma was doing that, Mary Ann and Maggie went into the kitchen. The radio was playing softly.

"I turned it on to see if they announced my sale," said Mary Ann. "I might have missed it. Now here is the lemon juice, and the pitcher, and some paper cups, and the sugar. The ice is in the top of the refrigerator."

"I can do it," said Maggie. "Don't you bother."

"I really am grateful," Mary Ann assured her. "I didn't expect any help. I didn't feel like asking the neighbors, they're all so busy and I don't know them too well." And she hurried out.

Maggie twiddled the knob on the radio. There was country music, and then local news. "Mr. and Mrs. Allen are having a yard sale today and tomorrow at the old Martin Farm on Hardscrabble Road in Broome Center. Sale starts at 10 A.M. Old furniture, kitchenware, tools and miscellaneous for sale."

Maggie was about to run to tell Mary Ann that her sale was on the radio, when the announcer went on: "Police are still looking for an old black station wagon, license number 303-NM2. A black wagon was last seen on the Taconic Parkway. It may have crossed the Rip Van Winkle bridge at Hudson. Bridge attendant seems to remember a black car driven by a man, not a woman, but as cars do not stop to pay toll going west, he paid little attention. Perhaps they were headed for a hideout in the mountains."

Maggie turned off the radio and ran out to the gas pump where Grandma was sitting and chatting with Tom.

"Grandma—" she began.

"Don't interrupt me, child," said Grandma. "Tom here is telling me a fascinating tale. He does wood carving, and he makes model furniture. You know, like for your dollhouse, only perfect models of antiques. He's invented a machine for making little chair legs—what is it, child?"

"There you are, ma'am," said Tom, going around to the back of the car and disconnecting the hose.

Maggie whispered urgently. "I just heard the radio. They're still looking for a black car. We better go."

"We can't go now. We have to help them."

"But all those people will come and they'll see a black car. What'll we do?"

"I know," said Grandma. "Mr. Allen, could I park someplace out of the way? I mean, you'll have a lot of people coming with cars and I don't want to be in the way."

"Fine," said Tom. "Just drive around behind the barn there."

Maggie breathed a sigh of relief. She jumped out and ran to the house, where Mary Ann was carrying a pile of books to the porch.

"Did you ever see so much stuff in one house?" she asked. "Oh, I hope somebody comes."

"I heard the man announce the sale on the radio," Maggie said.

"That's a relief," said Mary Ann. "I hope somebody was listening."

Grandma hurried across the yard. "I'll make the brownies if you want," she said. "People like some-thing to eat. They don't need it, most of them are too fat, but it makes them feel good, and if they bring kids, it keeps them quiet. Oh, that reminds me. Marcus, if people bring kids, let them draw with your Magic Mark-ers."

As Marcus looked doubtful, she went on, "Don't worry, I'll buy you some more. That's one thing that keeps little kids out of your hair, something to draw with."

By nine o'clock there was a fragrant smell of

brownies. By nine thirty, Laurie was sitting behind a card table ready to do business. Soon the people started to arrive. The first few were farmers' wives. They fingered the glassware and china.

One lady said, "Mary Ann, I always liked that red glass pickle dish of your grandmother's. But that's a high price you have on it."

Mary Ann, glancing over her shoulder at Grandma, said, "I know, Mrs. Harris, but it's a real old one. It's an antique. But I'll let you have it for half as you're an old friend." The lady walked off with her prize and Grandma whispered, "You're doing fine."

Another lady said, "I see you got some helpers, Mary Ann. Are they from away?"

"Oh, yes, Mrs. Brown, these are some of my friends from the city. They came to help me out. This lady made the brownies. Only we're going to run short."

Mrs. Brown remarked that she had just happened to make some of her nut cookies that morning. "I could bring some if you want."

"Oh, Mrs. Brown, that would be wonderful," said Mary Ann. "I'd be glad to trade you something. How about that cow pitcher you were looking at?"

"Oh, I'd love that, Mary Ann. I used to have one but my little boy broke it." And she hurried off to get the cookies.

Now a stream of cars began to arrive. Some people didn't buy anything, but others were heard to say to each other. "I didn't know there would be real antiques. I thought it was just some old farm-tool sale. I better phone my sister and tell her to get here."

"Better get more things out," said Grandma. "I'll go in the house and fix up the prices."

The yard was a scene of frantic activity. Tom and Marcus were carrying things to people's cars. Pedro was having the time of his life pumping gas. Laurie was selling lemonade and cookies. Maggie was keeping the children out of mischief, taking glassware out of their hands and giving them Magic Markers to draw with. Mary Ann and Grandma were dealing with the customers.

By four o'clock nearly everything was sold.

"What'll I do tomorrow?" Mary Ann asked worriedly.

"Haven't you got some pottery? And what about Tom's wood carvings? You could sell anything. You've got a talent for it. You ought to open a store."

Maggie said, "You could sell more cookies, I bet."

"Good thinking!" Grandma exclaimed. "We'll spend this evening baking. Run down to the store and buy up all their cake mixes and frosting. I don't believe in mixes but we can't be fussy."

"But Grandma—" Maggie began. She was wishing she hadn't mentioned cookies.

"Yes, you're right," said Grandma. "It's a little after four. We could still make it if we left now."

"But you *can't* leave now!" wailed Mary Ann. "You've worked all day, we haven't had supper. Where are you going, anyway? I never asked you."

"We're on our way to visit a cousin," Maggie explained. "She lives in Mountainside."

"But that's miles away. You better stay here tonight. We'll fix some supper."

"Nothing doing," said Tom. "We're going out to supper. The whole lot of us. Go on, wash up, everybody."

"What about Lucky?" Marcus asked. "Can I feed her?"

Mary Ann rummaged in the refrigerator and found some hamburger, which Lucky devoured in about two bites. Then she sat smiling and wagging her tail as if she was saying, "That was a nice snack, now where's my dinner?"

"We ought to buy her some dog food," Maggie said.

And Grandma added, "If we're going to bake cakes tonight, we better get busy and not go out to supper."

"Well, if that's how you feel," said Tom, "I'll drive to the village and get us a steak. You boys make a fire in the grill and have it going good by the time I get back. And put some potatoes in to bake."

"And don't forget the dog food. And some cake mixes," said Mary Ann.

Much later, all full of steak, buttered rolls, pickles, baked potatoes, ice cream and cherry pie, they sat in folding chairs around the still glowing grill, as if they were around a campfire. Lucky lay at Marcus' feet.

"If I only had my kitty!" Laurie whispered.

"Laurie!" said Maggie. "You know that kitty was wild and wanted to get away. She's happier in the barn. We'll get you one that will stay put. As soon as we get to Cousin Esther's."

"Now then," said Tom, "who's Cousin Esther? And suppose you tell us what brought you here and where you're going, and how did you just happen to pass here when you needed gas?"

78

"And we needed help," Mary Ann added.

Maggie and Grandma looked at each other. Was it safe to tell? They decided it was.

"You see," Maggie explained, "we're running away!"

Tom and Mary Ann listened as the whole incredible story came out.

"I can hardly believe it!" said Tom, when Maggie finished. "Putting Grandma in an old-age home! Why, she's worth the whole lot of us put together. That aunt of yours should be put in a mental institution."

"But the trouble is," said Maggie, "she'll get this doctor to sign a paper, and she'll get the social workers after Marcus and put him in a shelter, and Laurie won't be able to have a kitten, and now we've got Lucky, and we don't know whose she is—"

"She's mine," Marcus muttered under his breath.

"And the worst thing is that Aunt Ruby keeps after us. There was something on the radio this morning about the police looking for an old black wagon. That's when I came out and told Grandma and she moved it behind the barn."

"Well, you're safe here," said Mary Ann. "We have plenty of room—good thing we didn't sell the beds today. So you stay here with us as long as you like. Nobody will think to look on Hardscrabble Road for an old black station wagon."

"There's one thing I can't understand," said Maggie. "Why did the man say the car might be headed for a hideout in the mountains?"

Tom laughed. "That's where gangsters go. I don't think he means you."

It was dark now. The stars were shining in the black sky, and the coals in the grill had burned down to ashes. A whippoorwill called, and somewhere a bullfrog went *garonk! garonk!*

Laurie leaned heavily against Maggie's shoulder. She was sound asleep.

"We better put her to bed," said Maggie.

"We better all go to bed," Mary Ann said.

Tom picked up Laurie and carried her into the house. Pedro and Maggie took a flashlight and went to get their things out of the car. Mary Ann went to get sheets and towels.

Suddenly Grandma remembered something. "We have to bake cake," she said. "Where's the stuff you got in the store?"

"Grandma," said Maggie. "Come on. Let's go to bed. We'll get up at four o'clock tomorrow morning and have five hours to bake before the people come."

"Well, all right. I am a little bit sleepy," Grandma admitted.

SEVEN

It was five o'clock when Maggie, awakened by the sound of a rooster crowing far off, nudged Grandma gently.

"Get up, Grandma," she said.

"What for? Where am I? What are you bothering me for?" Grandma complained, brushing her away as if she were a persistent fly.

"We have to make cake for the sale. It was your idea, you know."

"Oh, yes. Why do I get these awful ideas?"

But she dragged herself out of bed.

"I'll go and make some coffee," said Maggie.

While the others slept, they began beating and mixing and putting pans in the oven, and soon the house was filled with such delectable odors that everyone else woke up and came down in pajamas to see what was going on. Grandma had saved the bowls for the children to lick.

"What about me?" Tom protested. "I haven't had a bowl to lick since I was ten. Mary Ann, why don't you ever make me a cake? I think what I need is a Grandma."

"Now, that's enough," Grandma exclaimed. "I'll give you the next one, right after breakfast."

Maggie made scrambled eggs and toast, and when Tom was given a plateful, he began to feel more cheerful.

"Now to work!" he proclaimed. "And don't forget my bowl!"

He and Pedro set up the tables with pottery, wood carvings and miniature furniture, plus what was left from yesterday's sale.

The women began frosting cakes, and Marcus had to make a new sign:

CRAFT AND CAKE SALE

By nine thirty the cars were again rolling in.

"What, no more antiques?" some people said. But instead they bought pottery and cake and went mad over Tom's dollhouse furniture. A number of customers insisted on giving him orders for more.

By afternoon nearly everything was gone and Tom and Mary Ann sat down on the porch steps to count their money and stack it in an old cigar box.

"I can't believe what we made!" said Mary Ann. "And we owe it all to you!"

Grandma and the children clustered around admiring the piles of money. "That's a beautiful sight," Grandma said. "Now I'll tell you what we'll do. After we have a little rest, we'll help you clean the place up a bit, and then we'll be on our way."

"We don't need to clean up right away," said Mary Ann.

"But you'll be having people come to look at the house," said Grandma. "You won't get a good price if they see it in a mess."

"Oh, but we're not selling!" said Mary Ann. "Didn't we tell you?"

"No! What happened?"

She explained. They had been so encouraged yesterday, they had made so much money and the neighbors had all been so friendly, that they were going to stay. Tom would open the repair shop, and in his spare time he would work on his wood carving and furniture, and Mary Ann would make her pottery, and maybe some friends would come and work with her. And Tom would try to get someone to help him in the shop.

"And so," Mary Ann concluded, "we wish you'd stay. If you don't want to stay in the house, we can fix up the barn. There's lots of space there. We could partition off some rooms—"

Maggie looked at Grandma. She could see her eyes beginning to twinkle.

"It would be great," Maggie said quickly, "but we have to get to Cousin Esther's."

"Of course," said Grandma, "she doesn't know we're coming. Nobody knows where we are."

"But sooner or later somebody will hear the radio and report us and then Aunt Ruby will catch up with us."

"Wait a minute," said Pedro. "I got an idea. What does the radio say? They looking for a black wagon with number 303-NM2. Well, we don't got 303-NM2. We got 70-PKF. That's one thing. But our get-away car, she's black, right? Well, we paint her blue. Then nobody knows."

They all stared at him in admiration. What a simple, yet brilliant idea!

"Of course!" said Tom. "And it just so happens I have two cans of paint in the garage. Only they're green."

"Green is okay," said Pedro.

"But she's Mr. Ramon's car," said Maggie. "Maybe he won't like it to be green."

"He'll like it," said Pedro. "Don't worry."

"The first thing tomorrow we start," said Tom. "Tonight we go out to eat."

Saturday, Tom and Pedro worked happily on the car. They had to sand it down, take off the dirt and rust and grease, and then wash it. They replaced Pedro's string with wire and tuned up the motor.

Meanwhile Grandma, Maggie and Mary Ann tidied the house.

"I love it," said Mary Ann joyfully. "It's so nice with all that old stuff out of it. I realize now why I hated it. It was so cluttered. I'm going to paint the walls white and have no curtains—maybe a few pictures but that's all. I might even paint the pictures right on the walls."

Marcus heard this and said shyly, "You want me to paint some pictures?"

"Can you paint?" Mary Ann asked.

"Uh-huh," said Marcus.

"Well, go ahead. Try it."

Marcus got out his Magic Markers. He said, "I start in the back room. Then if you don't like it you can paint over it."

Soon he was blissfully drawing a mural all across one wall. Lucky sat and watched him, though it was hard to see how she could be a good art critic with hair all over her eyes. As he drew, he talked to her.

"You like this, Lucky? See what it is? It's all about our trip. See, this is where we started, in the city. You weren't there. We got you later."

Lucky wagged her tail approvingly.

"Marcus, it's wonderful!" Mary Ann exclaimed. "You're an artist." And she called the others to come and look.

Marcus, his face red with embarrassment, scuffed his feet and said, "Aw, it's nothing."

"Monday we'll get white paint for the living room. When it's clean you can decorate on top."

In the late afternoon, Grandma and Maggie went for a walk. Maggie wanted to get Grandma away from the housecleaning for a while. "Look, Grandma," she said, "there's a path out beyond the barn. Let's see where it goes."

The path led to a brook that gurgled over rocks and pebbles. Beside the brook was a grassy spot where they sat down. There were wild strawberries in the grass, and they picked and ate some.

"I bet there are fish in that brook," said Grandma. "I used to be a good hand with a fishing line. I had a boyfriend named Hank. We used to go fishing. I'll see if Tom has any tackle. You know, Maggie, this is a good place. I'm glad those young people are staying. They just needed a little encouragement. Come on, let's see about the fishing."

"You stay here," said Maggie. "I'll go."

Grandma stretched out on the grass while Maggie ran back to the house. There she was horrified to see Mary Ann talking to a man in a wide-brimmed hat with a gun holster on his belt. A police car stood in the driveway.

"Well, thanks anyway, Miz Allen," the policeman was saying. "We got this report and I just thought I'd check it out."

"It's all right, Officer," said Mary Ann. "Of course we want to help if we can. If I see a black car I'll call you right away. What's the license number now? I'll write it down. 303-NM2."

The policeman lifted his hat, put it back on, and drove away. Mary Ann and Maggie walked out behind the garage. There stood a bright green car.

Tom and Pedro came out grinning.

"How you like her?" Pedro demanded. "Pretty good, hah?"

"Not finished yet," said Tom. "We still have to do the other side. But if that cop had looked this way, this is the side he would have seen."

"It's great!" said Maggie. "Wait till Grandma sees it! Oh, I almost forgot. Have you any fishing tackle?"

Supper that night was fresh-caught fish and berries. There were also canned peaches and green tomato pickles. Grandma had suggested that Mary Ann look in the cellar in case her grandmother had put up garden things. Sure enough there were still a few jars left.

Tom decreed that the car could not be driven until it had stood for a couple of days, to give the paint a chance to harden. Besides, he said, Sunday was to be a day of rest, since they had all worked so hard. Rest consisted of playing baseball and swimming in the brook, taking along soap and towels at Grandma's orders.

Then on Monday they had to go shopping for white paint, and the living room had to be painted, and Marcus spent Tuesday decorating it.

But on Wednesday morning, Grandma said firmly, "Well, this is it. I'm sorry, but we have to go. I just remembered I promised to phone Mr. Ramon when we got to Esther's, and he must think we're lost or arrested or something. So come on, kids."

Pedro scowled. "Why we got to go?" he demanded. "It's nice here."

"He's right," said Mary Ann.

But Grandma shook her head. "That cop the other day was nice. But he'd get suspicious if he heard any more reports. Then Tom and Mary Ann would be in trouble. So get ready."

Pedro scowled more fiercely. "I don't wanna go," he said. "If I get back to the city, they make me go to work in a grocery store. And you know, Grandma, this is only your vacation. You not out here for good."

Tom said, "But why not? Don't go. Stay here. But if

you can't all stay, just leave Pedro. I need him. He can have a job pumping gas, and he can help fix cars, and I'll teach him math and science. Then in September he can go to school."

There was complete silence as they took in what Tom had said. Pedro broke it. "You mean, you want me to stay here with you?"

"Sure, that's what I said," said Tom. "Right, Mary Ann?"

"It's the only thing," said Mary Ann. "Tom needs a helper and you want to stay, so it's settled. If Grandma agrees."

Pedro looked into Grandma's eyes. Very earnestly he said, "Grandma, you like my own family. If you want me to stay, I stay. But if you say no, I obey you."

There was doubt in Grandma's eyes. After all, Pedro was only fourteen. And she had known the Allens only a few days. But she couldn't resist the pleading in his voice.

"It's all right with me," she said, "but what about his family? They'll be wondering where he is. What will I tell them? Can you take care of him?"

"We'll write them a letter," Tom said. "We'll phone them and tell them where we are. Then we'll write to you and tell you what they say. If it's okay with them, he can stay."

"All right," said Grandma. "On one condition. Pedro, you write me a letter once a month, so I'll know how you're doing."

Pedro's scowl disappeared. Instead there was a broad grin on his face and he leaped in the air yelling like a

Comanche Indian. "Yippee! I'm gonna stay! I got me a job!"

Then he calmed down and said soberly, "But I'm sorry you won't be here too, all you guys. You like my brothers and sisters. I write to you too."

"Okay, Pedro," said Maggie. "And we'll write to you. What's the address? Broome Center, New York." She held out her hand. Pedro took it. Then he leaned over and kissed her on the cheek. Then, his face scarlet with embarrassment, he rushed off into the barn.

At last they were on their way.

"Don't know if I can get used to driving a green car," said Grandma. "I might get off the road now and then."

"Oh, no, you won't!" said Maggie. "Not this time. Tom marked the map for us. Now we go north on this road."

They proceeded for about an hour. Then Grandma saw a side road.

"I wonder where that goes," she said.

"Grandma!" Maggie said severely. "Sometimes I don't think you really want to go to Cousin Esther's."

Grandma said, "Well, I haven't seen her in years. Maybe we should have written first."

"We couldn't, remember?" said Maggie. "We had no time."

"That's true." They drove on in silence for a bit. "Maybe she won't be there." Silence again. "It's been a week now," said Grandma suddenly. "Maybe we should go back. I do have to get back to my job, you know."

"Are we broke, Grandma?" Maggie asked.

"I don't have much money left," said Grandma. "This car is a real gas-guzzler. Of course maybe Esther can lend me some. If she's there."

Suddenly Marcus, who hadn't said a word all morning, announced: "I don't wanna go home. They'll take Lucky away and put me in a shelter."

"Oh, I don't think so," said Grandma. "Not as long as I'm your foster grandmother." But she sounded uncertain, and she drove slowly and carefully. Gone was the reckless gaiety with which she had started out.

Maggie felt a pang of fear. It wasn't like Grandma to be so doubtful. She sounded—well, a little scared. In another moment she might say, "You better go live with Aunt Ruby after all." Maggie wished they would get there soon. Grandma would be safe with Cousin Esther, and then they would all be safe.

She decided to change the subject. "I'm hungry," she announced. "Let's stop and have lunch. We have those sandwiches you made, and we'll get some milk in that store up ahead and ask how far it is to Mountainside. You stay here. I'll go."

She was afraid that if Grandma got talking to the person in the store she would start helping behind the counter. In the store she knew her intuition had been correct. There was a mother cat with three kittens, and the man in charge was trying to run the store and take care of two small children at once.

Maggie bought the milk and asked where Mountainside was.

"Why, you're almost in it," the man replied. "Just go down this road till you come to a T. Turn right, go down the hill and around a bend, and there you are."

"Thank you," said Maggie, hurrying out before any of the others could come after her.

They ate lunch sitting in the car, parked by the roadside under a huge tree.

"That's a nice tree," said Marcus, looking up at its spreading branches.

"It's a maple," said Grandma. "A sugar maple. Lots of them around here."

"Do you get sugar from a tree?" Laurie asked.

"In March," Grandma said, "we used to tap the trees. We'd fasten a bucket on the tree and the sap would drip into it. Then we collected all the sap and boiled it down to make syrup."

"Wow!" said Marcus. "I didn't know trees could do that."

He took out his green Magic Marker and started drawing on the bag in which Maggie had brought the milk. He outlined the shape of the maple. Under the tree sat Lucky, smiling.

"Look what he's doing, Grandma," said Maggie.

Grandma looked and nodded. "Yes," she said, "we'll have to go on. We can't go back now."

"Why did you say that?"

"That boy's got talent. If we take him back to his uncle, that will kill it."

They packed the remains of the lunch and set off. Soon they came to the T, and then they began to see houses, set far apart on wide lawns.

"We're coming to the village," said Grandma. "It begins to look familiar."

EIGHT

"I just can't get over it! Back here after all those years!"

They were on the main street of the village. Cars were parked on a slant along the curb. People were walking along the sidewalk calmly, as if nothing unusual were happening.

"There's the post office!" said Grandma. "And the bank. But where's Mr. Waddell's grocery store, and where's Miss Dinkins' Ladies' Shoppe?"

"There's a doughnut shop," said Laurie. "I love doughnuts."

"We can't stop now," Maggie began. But Grandma pulled up to the curb. "Yes, let's stop," she said. "We'll buy some doughnuts to take to Esther. And we'll ask the way. I'm not sure I remember."

She went into the shop and came out carrying a box and looking annoyed.

"I asked if Esther Crouse ever came in there and they said they never heard of her!"

"What's strange about that?" Maggie asked.

Grandma gave her a pitying glance. "You were raised in the city," she said, "where you hardly know your next-door neighbor. But here everybody knows everybody. Or they used to. Here, have a doughnut."

"Maybe it's changed," Maggie suggested. "The doughnut shop looks new."

"Can we get out of the car?" Laurie asked.

"And can I take Lucky out?" said Marcus.

"Yes, go for a walk. I must think what to do."

Marcus and Laurie walked up the street with Lucky. In a few minutes they were back.

"There's a paper store," said Marcus. "Could I buy some new Magic Markers? Mine are all used up."

Grandma went with him. "Well, that looks familiar," she said, as they entered. Inside, a wrinkled old man sat behind the counter. "Well, if it isn't Hank Duffy!"

The old man blinked at her.

"Don't you remember me? I'm Susan Miklusky. Susan Crouse that was. You used to take me fishing."

He leaned forward and peered at her.

"And this is my granddaughter Maggie. Lizzie's daughter."

"You don't say! She doesn't favor Lizzie. Looks more dark."

"That's right. Lizzie was blonde like me."

"You don't look blonde," the old man said. "And I remember Susan was a skinny little thing."

"Well, people change," said Grandma. "You certainly have. But tell me, how is Esther? Do you see her?"

"Esther Crouse? Oh sure. See her most every day. Why?"

"We came to visit," said Grandma. "But I can't just remember the way to the house."

The old man said, "Why, you just go down Main and turn right at the corner, and then past the church, then left and then right again. Reckon you won't stay long."

"Why not? Is she sick, or something?"

"Oh, no, she's good and strong. You'll see." Suddenly he shouted, "What's that boy doing? No dogs allowed in here!"

At his shout Lucky whirled around, knocking over a rack of magazines with her tail.

"Now look what you did!" the old man scolded.

The children began picking up the magazines.

"Stop fussing," Grandma said. "Marcus is with me. He wants some Magic Markers. Go ahead, Marcus, pick out what you want. Get a whole set. And how about some paper to draw on?"

She seemed to have cheered up considerably since finding someone she knew.

"Gee, that would be neat," Marcus said.

Grandma pulled an assortment of art materials from the shelves, including a coloring book and some crayons for Laurie.

"There! See the kittens? That should keep you quiet for a while. Now then, Hank, what do I owe you?"

"That'll be four dollars and seventy-three cents," said Mr. Duffy.

"That's robbery," said Grandma.

"Well, things have changed since you were here," he said. "But I'll let you have it for four fifty."

Maggie said, "Come on, Grandma, let's not buy anything else." She didn't want Grandma to start buying a big box of candy for Cousin Esther. They left the store and climbed into the car. Grandma backed jauntily out of her parking place, nearly crashing into an oncoming car which hooted madly.

"What's wrong with these people?" she said. "What are they so excited about?"

They drove along a street lined with white houses, some of them big old-fashioned ones with wooden lace and turrets. There were green lawns and pretty flower gardens. It must be wonderful, Maggie thought, to live in one of them. Cousin Esther's must be like them. She could hardly wait to see the white-painted garden seats, the ring of seashells, and the pond with the ducks.

They turned left, then right. Grandma drove slowly.

"It's in here somewhere," she said. They passed a wooded area and then a row of little cottages.

"Those are new," said Grandma. "I never saw them before. Where is Esther's house? That Hank Duffy must have been fooling me."

"Let's stop and ask," Maggie said. "There's a woman. Ask her."

Grandma shouted, "Do you know where Miss Crouse lives?"

The woman shook her head.

Maggie said, "I'll get out and look."

She walked along the pavement looking at the letter

boxes. Each house had one on a post near the sidewalk. The names were painted on them: Smith, Jones, Robinson.

In front of the wooded area was an old rusty box that seemed ready to fall down. The name on it was Crouse.

"I found it!" she called out. "In here!" She peered through the bushes. There was a driveway, not like the neat blacktopped ones the other houses had, but full of ruts and stones. She walked up it. There was a house in there, but so hidden by trees that she could hardly see it. She came running back to the car.

"There's a house," she announced, "but I don't know if anybody is home. I didn't go to the door. It's scary."

Grandma parked the car by the curb, and they all got out and went up the driveway together, leaving Lucky in the car.

"Better not bring her in till we see what's what," she said.

They passed a battered car. There were two rusty iron garden seats, one on each side of a ring of shells, but there were no flowers growing in the ring, only a few dried up stalks. The trees and bushes grew like jungle plants. Bittersweet and Virginia creeper climbed up them like ropes.

The house, they now saw, was covered with dark brown shingles. There was a porch around it, but one end of it was falling down, and the steps leading up to it were rickety. Bottles and cans lay in a heap on the ground. Maggie was right. It was scary.

"My land a living!" Grandma exclaimed, staring around. "How did it get like this? It used to be so pretty.

It was like a showplace, the only house on this side of the street."

Laurie edged closer and slipped her hand into Maggie's. Marcus gazed in astonishment. He had seen street alleys but he had never seen anything like this.

"Hey, it looks like a movie I saw once," he began. "There was this creepy place—"

"Never mind that," Grandma interrupted. She marched up the steps and knocked loudly at the door. The children waited. There was no answer. She tried the door. It was locked. Then she banged.

There was a sound of feet coming slowly, and the key turned in the lock. The door opened with a creak. An old woman stood there, small and skinny with white curly hair that stuck out all around her head. Her face was brown and wrinkled. She wore sneakers, dungarees and a plaid flannel shirt several sizes too big.

"What you want?" she demanded in a cross voice. "I haven't got nothing for you."

"Esther!" said Grandma. "Don't you know me?"

"No, I don't!" said the woman. "What's your name?"

"I'm Susie," said Grandma.

The woman peered at her. "Susie? Sure enough? You put on weight then."

"And you took some off," said Grandma. "Well, aren't you going to invite us in?"

"Who's us? Who are those kids? I don't want kids here."

"This is Maggie, my granddaughter. And these are Laurie and Marcus. They're our neighbors. We took them for a little trip."

Cousin Esther said, "Oh! I thought they were just some strange kids. Pesky kids are always bothering me."

Grandma said, somewhat impatiently, "Well, can we come in?"

"Oh, yes," said Esther. "Come on in. But be careful of the floor. Some loose boards there."

They followed her through a dark hall. Maggie had a glimpse of rooms opening on either side, and stairs going up. The rooms seemed to be cluttered with stuff.

At the end of the hall was the kitchen. And what a kitchen! There was an iron sink, a big black stove with a pipe going though the ceiling, a smaller stove, a table cluttered with cans and dishes, some shelves with assorted dishes and glassware, some of them dusty and broken.

Grandma seemed to be speechless. Maggie was amazed. Was this the lovely house they had come so far to find?

Finally Grandma said, "Well, Esther, I wouldn't have known the old house."

Esther said, "I guess I haven't kept it up too good. I been busy."

"Are you all alone?"

"Oh, sure, except for the cats."

"Cats!" said Laurie. "Where are they?"

As if in answer, a handsome black cat came in. He jumped on the table, landing on all four feet without disturbing a single dish, sat down and gazed at them with yellow eyes. A gray cat with white feet appeared, sniffed at a dish on the floor, and walking over to Cousin Esther, rubbed against her ankles.

"What's wrong with that food?" Cousin Esther demanded. "Ever since she had kittens, she's been fussy about what she'll eat."

"Kittens!" sighed Laurie, blissfully. They had come to the right place. "Where are they?"

"Oh, they're around someplace," said Esther. "I better feed her. I got to go to work."

"Work!" said Grandma. "This is a funny time to go to work. Where do you work?"

"In the bank," said Esther, starting to open cans of cat food.

"What do you do there?"

"What? Oh, I clean. After three o'clock when the bank closes."

Grandma said, "Well, we'll stay here and wait till you come back. When will that be?"

"About five," said Esther. "Where you staying?"

"Staying?" exclaimed Grandma. "We came to see you. Haven't you got room for us? There used to be about ten rooms in this house, plus the attic."

"Yes, well, some of them are pretty full of stuff," Esther said doubtfully. "But I'll see when I get back."

She went out and climbed into the beat-up old car, and soon they heard a clanking, grinding noise as the car backed down the driveway.

NINE

Maggie looked around doubtfully. "Can we stay here, Grandma?" she asked.

Grandma said, "Well, it sure isn't what I expected."

"You said she was rich. I thought her house would be pretty, like the other houses."

"Sure has gone downhill," said Grandma. "I can't understand it. Aunt Ida never would have put up with it. But I guess what happened, Aunt Ida died. Then Cousin Bertha died. That left Esther all alone and she just couldn't handle it. You'd think the neighbors would give her a hand."

"Maybe she doesn't know the neighbors," said Maggie.

"I told you, out here everybody knows their neighbors. She doesn't talk to them, most likely. Well, there's only one thing to do—clean it up."

Maggie looked around at the messy kitchen. "Okay," she said, "I'll wash the dishes."

"I'll dry," said Laurie.

Grandma opened the cupboard and investigated its contents. "Not much food in here. Mostly cat food and soup. Wonder what she eats."

Maggie began to gather up the dirty dishes that lay in heaps all over the table and counter.

"Find something and dump out these empty cans," she told Marcus. "Then see if you can find a broom."

But when she went to the sink, she found there was no hot water.

"How do you wash dishes here?" she asked.

"I guess you have to heat water on the stove," said Grandma.

Maggie examined the big black stove. "This? How does it work?"

"I guess she doesn't use that one in summer. We used to use it in winter. Heated up the whole room. In summer she must use the oil stove over there."

She opened a little door on the front of the stove, struck a match, and lit a wick that burned with a blue flame. Maggie filled a kettle and put it on to heat.

Meanwhile Marcus swept the floor and Laurie wandered out into the hall.

Maggie, waiting for the kettle to heat, stood at the back door. Something out there said, "Quack, quack!" There were two ducks, paddling in an old bathtub sunk into the ground. When they saw her they got out of the water and waddled over to the wire fence, quacking loudly.

"Ducks!" said Grandma, hearing them. "We always used to have ducks. Wonder what happened to their pond. Here, give them this bread, it's too stale to eat."

Maggie threw the bread over the fence and the ducks gobbled it up. Then she went back and tackled the dishes. After an hour or so, the kitchen, while not exactly clean, was a bit tidier.

"Where do you think we can sleep, Grandma?" Maggie asked.

"There are plenty of bedrooms," said Grandma. "Let's look."

They peered into the living room, which Maggie had glimpsed from the hall. It was a bedroom now. There was a couch in the corner, where Cousin Esther obviously slept, for it was covered with rumpled sheets and blankets. And in the middle of it was Laurie, blissfully cuddling a family of kittens.

"I found the kittens," she whispered. "They're asleep. Don't wake them up."

"Well, she's happy at last," said Grandma. "Let's see, what's in here?"

In here was the dining room, with a round oak table, a huge sideboard and massive chairs. It was a gloomy room. Dust lay everywhere.

"I remember all of us sitting around that table for Sunday dinner," Grandma mused. "Aunt Ida would bring in the roast from the kitchen and Uncle Isaac would carve. He had a long white beard. Sometimes it would get in the gravy. We almost died trying not to laugh."

They climbed the stairs, which creaked protestingly at each step. Opening off a central hall were several bedrooms. One had a double bed with a faded lavender spread, and ragged lace curtains. The room was dark.

"Pull up the shades, Maggie," said Grandma. But there were no shades. Vines growing over the windows kept the light out. The other bedrooms were crammed with stuff—boxes of books and old magazines and heaps of clothes piled on the beds.

"My goodness, this is terrible!" said Grandma. "I don't know how Esther can live like this. She needs help. I wish we could stay and straighten her out."

"But Grandma," said Maggie. "Your job—"

"Yes, well, I have another week of vacation coming. Maybe I'll phone my boss and see if I can stay."

"What's up there?" Marcus asked, pointing to the stair that led up to a closed door.

"That's the attic," said Grandma. "We won't go up there now. I don't think I could stand it. Let's go down."

"I better get Lucky out of the car," said Marcus. "I bet she's tired of sitting there."

"I'll go with you," said Maggie. "Grandma, you sit down and take a rest."

"All right, maybe I will. Think I'll make some tea. I'm a little hungry. Bring those doughnuts when you come back."

Marcus ran down the driveway to the car. Maggie followed more slowly. It wasn't quite as scary as it had seemed at first. Still, it was dark and gloomy under the trees. There were noises. A chattering sound—that was a squirrel. Maggie could see him in a tree, scolding at them. And a rustling sound as if something was moving through the underbrush.

Then a voice said, "Who is it? Doesn't sound like our guys."

"Search me," said another voice.

"Who's there?" Maggie called loudly.

Two girls appeared from behind the bushes. They wore jeans and T-shirts. One had long blonde hair and the other short black hair.

"Who are you?" the blonde one asked. "Is that your car out there with the dog in it?"

Maggie admitted it was.

"Your folks going to buy the place?"

"No, of course not," said Maggie.

"Well, what are you doing here when Esther's out?"

"How do you know she's out?"

"Her car is gone." This was a new idea to Maggie. She had never thought of looking to see if a car was gone to know if someone was home or not.

"We're visiting her. She's my grandmother's cousin."

"Oh! We didn't know she had any folks."

"Well, she has. And what did you come for?" (Maggie remembered Esther's remarks about pesky kids.)

The blonde one said, "Should we tell?"

Maggie said, "You better tell. If you're doing anything she wouldn't like—"

"Oh, go ahead and tell," said the dark one. "It's nothing really. We're looking for treasure."

"Treasure! What kind of treasure?"

"Oh, not gold or money. Just glass bottles. We call it treasure. Some of those old bottles are valuable, but she wouldn't care. See, she buries them."

"*Buries* them!"

"Sure, didn't you know? She doesn't have her trash collected, she just digs a hole and buries it."

The dark girl said, "They say she won't be here much longer, so we thought we better dig now. Once I found an arrowhead."

"Why won't she be here?"

"Oh, because she's getting old and the place is a health hazard. There are rats, they say."

Just then Marcus appeared with Lucky. He had tied a rope around her neck for a leash and she was gamboling happily about like a huge woolly sheep.

"Who's that?" the blonde girl asked. "Is he with you? Oh, what a beautiful dog! I just love English sheepdogs." And she buried her hands in Lucky's fur. Lucky licked her nose.

"Is that what she is?" said Marcus.

"Marcus!" Maggie said. "This girl says there are rats here. By the way, I'm Maggie Fisher, what's your name?"

The blonde girl was Liz, the dark one was Judy. They said that besides the rats, the neighbors were worried about fire, since Esther used kerosene. They said she ought to be in an old-age home.

"But don't tell her we said so," said Judy. "I kind of feel sorry for her. And my mother does too. She cleans for my mom, and Mom gives her things, clothes, you know, or food. But the neighbors are getting mad. They say this place spoils the neighborhood."

"Hey!" Liz said, grabbing her friend's arm. "Here she comes. I can tell her car a mile off." They disappeared into the bushes.

Cousin Esther's car bumped and rattled over the rocks and stopped. She got out and hoisted out a shopping bag. Maggie and Marcus tried to help her.

"Where did that dog come from?" she demanded crossly.

"It's ours," Maggie said.

"Well, you can't bring it in the house."

"Okay," said Marcus. "I'll tie her up out here. She'll be a good watchdog in case anybody comes. And if she sees a rat she can scare it away."

"Rats! Who said anything about rats?" Esther asked.

"Nobody. He means squirrels," said Maggie.

They followed Esther into the kitchen, where Grandma was stacking dishes in the cupboard.

"Well, Susie, what do you think you're doing?" Esther shouted.

Grandma turned around and the two old ladies glared at each other.

"Esther," Grandma said, "you always were messy but I never thought to see you living in a pigsty."

"Is that so!" cried Esther, her frizzy hair shaking with anger. "I'll thank you to mind your own business. What did you come for anyway? After all those years! Did anybody say anything about me?"

"No, Esther," Grandma replied. "Calm down. I just wanted to see you. But if you don't want us we can go to a motel. Or maybe some of my friends can put us up. I saw Hank Duffy down to the store."

"What he tell you about me?"

"He said we wouldn't stay long, if you must know."

The children stood by, listening uneasily.

Finally Maggie asked, "Should I unpack this bag, Cousin Esther?"

Esther whirled around and glared angrily. "What's that?" Then she said sulkily, "Oh, sure! Just a few things I got for supper. I see your grandma has throwed out a lot of stuff so there's room in the closet."

"I just threw out some moldy bread and dried out bottles," said Grandma. "But I'm sorry if you needed them."

"It's all right," said Esther. "And I guess you can sleep here. I'll have to clear out a couple of rooms."

Grandma said, "Marcus can sleep in the dining room, and we girls can sleep in that bedroom with the lavender spread. That was Bertha's room, wasn't it? Sorry if I butted in to what wasn't my business."

Laurie appeared with three kittens in her arms, their tiny claws clinging to her shirt.

"I like this place," she said. "Can I feed them? They're hungry and their mother went away and left them."

"I guess she saw you were going to take over," said Esther. "Here's some milk. They're about ready to drink. And I guess we can eat pretty soon. I got some beans and franks and we can have coffee and cake. You sure cleaned up the place," she added grudgingly. "Thanks. I been meaning to do it but I been busy."

"Lucky is hungry too," said Marcus.

"Go bring her in," said Grandma. "Don't worry, Esther, she's a real nice dog. She won't hurt the cats."

When Lucky was brought in, the kittens prepared to defend their lives or die fighting, but when Lucky lay down and pretended to be a woolly rug, they approached and were soon climbing on top of her. Esther admitted she wasn't a bad dog, as dogs went.

Maggie went out to get a can of dog food from the car.

"Better bring the blankets and the bags with the pajamas," Grandma said. "And the flashlights."

Supper was over. Lucky had licked the plates clean, and now lay on the floor with her nose between her paws. The three kittens nestled against her. Laurie was curled up on the couch at the end of the kitchen with the black cat purring loudly in her arms. Grandma and Cousin Esther were drinking coffee. Marcus was drawing on a paper bag. Maggie started to put the dishes in the sink, but decided to wait. There was a peaceable silence and she didn't want to break it.

At last Esther said, "Well, Susie, come on. What's on your mind?"

Grandma said, "I told you. Maggie was asking about you. It was time for my vacation, so I thought we'd drive out and pay a visit."

"But you didn't write. Most people write and ask if they can come."

"We wanted to phone, but we didn't know the number."

"No. I haven't got a phone."

Maggie decided they had had enough of beating around the bush.

"We had no time to write," she burst out. "We had to get away fast. See, Aunt Ruby was after us. She wants to take me away and send me to school in California. She's mean. She wants to put Grandma in a home."

"And we won't let her," said Laurie from the couch.

"Grandma takes care of us," said Marcus, drawing faster on the bag. "She's a nice lady."

"So we got out," said Maggie. "We didn't know where to go so I said, let's go see your cousin. Because, see, Grandma used to tell me stories about you and your house, how nice it was. And I said, if Cousin Esther has a house she must be rich, maybe we can stay with her awhile."

Esther began to laugh. She laughed so hard that Maggie thought she would choke. She jumped up and patted her on the back.

"I'm okay," gasped Esther. "You thought I was rich, ha-ha! And you came here and found a dump! Well, what a surprise for you! What are you going to do now?"

Grandma said, "We'll have to go back to the city. The only trouble is, we ran out of cash. I was hoping you'd lend me some."

Esther started to laugh again, but stopped.

"You know what?" she said. "When I saw you, the first thought I had was, you'd lend *me* some money."

Maggie asked, "Cousin Esther, is it true what those kids said?"

Esther started up angrily. "What kids? I can't make those kids stay away from here—"

"Some kids were looking for bottles," said Maggie. "They said there were rats here."

"There's no rats! That's just a lie to get me out. They made me fill in the duck pond, said it brought mosquitoes. Now they want to tear down the house and build a lot of new ones. It's those real-estate people. They want to buy it cheap and make a profit. So they say it's a hazard and a disgrace to the neighborhood."

Grandma observed, "Well, you must admit it doesn't look too nice. And it used to be so pretty."

"Well, I can't keep it up the way Papa did. But I don't bother anybody. Only I'm behind on the taxes. I'll lose it this year if I can't pay up."

Her face grew sad and she twisted her hands together.

Grandma said, "Why don't you sell it then? It must be worth quite a bit."

"And go live in an old folks' home?" said Esther. "Along with you?"

The two old women stared at each other and began to laugh again.

"You've got a point, Esther," said Grandma. "Well, we better get together. Maybe we can work something out. Marcus, stop drawing. It's too dark. Maggie, turn on the light."

Maggie had been noticing that it was getting dark but hadn't wanted to mention it. Now she got up and pushed a switch. Nothing happened.

Esther took a glass lamp off a shelf and lit it.

"Haven't you got any electric?" Grandma asked.

"Never use it," said Esther, as if it were some kind of bad habit. "Had it turned off about five years ago. I like this better."

And indeed the lamp spread a gentle glow over the table, hiding the dust and cobwebs in the corners of the room.

Grandma said, "Remember when we used to come in here and make fudge? My, that was good. And popcorn on the big stove. And Aunt Ida yelled at us for using too much butter. And we played records on the phonograph and danced. I see you still have that wind-up phonograph. You still have any of those records?"

"Sure, got 'em all. I play them sometimes when I can't sleep."

Maggie asked, "Haven't you got a radio?"

"No, and no TV either. Can't use 'em without electric."

Suddenly Maggie said, "We haven't listened to the radio in two days. I wonder if they're still looking for that car. You see," she explained, "we borrowed this old black car from our super. We called it our get-away car. Then we heard that the cops were looking for it. We figured Aunt Ruby was after us, so we painted it green. Cousin Esther, have you got a newspaper?"

Esther said, "I picked up one a couple of days ago that somebody had throwed out. It's over on the big stove."

Marcus picked it up and started to turn the pages.

Suddenly he yelled, "Hey!"

"What? Is it something about the car?"

"No! Look at that!"

There was a picture of a dog, a big woolly sheepdog with hair all over its face. The lines underneath said:

> This is Josephine. She was lost or stolen from a home in Scarsdale a week ago. If you find her, phone us. $300 reward and no questions asked.

There was a name, address and phone number.

Marcus' face was white. He looked afraid, as he had when he thought the social worker was coming to get him.

"What's wrong, Marcus?" Maggie asked.

"Nothing, I was afraid that was Lucky. But it couldn't be. We didn't go near that place. And her name isn't Josephine, is it, Lucky?"

Lucky got up and wagged her tail. Maggie grabbed the paper. "Three hundred dollars!"

"Your name is Lucky," said Marcus. "Right, Lucky?"

The dog wagged her tail and licked his nose.

He looked around angrily. "See?"

Maggie said, "Maybe somebody stole her and took her on the parkway and she got out of the car and got lost. We could get three hundred dollars!"

"No!" said Marcus. "She's my dog. Come on, Lucky."

"Where are you going?"

"Going to bed, me and Lucky." And he marched off to the dining room.

"He hasn't got anything to sleep on," said Esther. "Go get him some cushions from the other room."

Maggie ran after him. "Take these, Marcus," she said. "And here's a blanket."

"I'm all right," he muttered. "Leave me alone. Me and Lucky can get along."

And he lay down on the floor and pulled the blanket over himself and the dog.

TEN

"Poor Marcus," said Grandma. "He's never had anything of his own. And now he has Lucky."

"But Grandma," said Maggie, "even if we don't find the owner, how can he keep her?"

"It's a problem," Grandma admitted. "We can't solve it tonight. It's time for bed. Where's Laurie?"

Laurie was sound asleep on the couch, with three kittens in her arms. "Might as well let her stay there." She took the candle Esther gave her and led the way upstairs.

Lying in the big bed watching Grandma's shadow as she undressed, Maggie thought, What are we going to do now?

Grandma echoed her thought. "Everybody has problems. Poor old Esther. Hers are worse than ours."

She blew out the candle and climbed into bed.

Faintly, in the darkness, Maggie heard music, soft and far away. It was Esther, playing her old records.

"Maybe tomorrow we'll think of something," she said.

When Maggie woke up it was still dark, though it seemed as if it must be morning. She heard noises from downstairs. She looked at the window. Oh, yes, it was the vines on the outside that shut out the light. Grandma was still asleep, snoring gently. Carefully, so as not to waken her, Maggie got out of bed, pulled her clothes on, and headed for the stairs. But first she peered into the other rooms. They were full of a strange assortment of stuff—old clothes, shoes, pocketbooks, plastic flowers, boxes of buttons, old curtains. What on earth did Cousin Esther want with all that stuff?

She looked up at the attic door and wondered what was behind it. Why not look? She tiptoed up the stairs and opened the door. It was a huge attic, the full width of the house. The only light came from a window at each end. In the semidarkness she could see furniture—chairs, chests, trunks, a spinning wheel. Propped against one of the chests was something covered with a rug. She lifted the rug and saw some pictures in carved frames.

She bent down and squinted at the outside one. It was a painting of a house with a garden around it. In the garden there seemed to be a ring of shells, and a white-painted seat. But it was so dim in the attic that she couldn't be sure.

She covered it up again and picked her way to the window at one end of the attic. Looking down, she could see the tangle of trees, and beyond that the street and some neighbors' houses with neat lawns and trimmed hedges.

Far off, she heard a bark. There was Marcus running along the driveway with Lucky.

"I better go down," she thought.

When she reached the kitchen, Laurie and Marcus were there, pouring corn flakes into bowls. Marcus was giving every other flake to Lucky who sat with her mouth open in a wide smile.

"I never knew before that dogs could smile," said Maggie. "She's nice."

"Yeah! And she's mine," Marcus declared.

"And Esther says I can have a kitten," said Laurie happily. "I can't decide whether to take the black one or the gray one. You think I could have both?"

Maggie almost wanted to cry, looking at the two of them. How could they go back to a small city apartment with a kitten and a sheepdog? And even if they did, how long could Marcus and Laurie stay with her and Grandma? Somebody would drag them off somewhere. If they could only stay here in this big house, with Cousin Esther!

"Where is Cousin Esther, by the way?" she asked.

"She went to work someplace," said Laurie.

Maggie buttered a piece of bread and went outside the back door to eat it. She wanted to think. But the ducks spotted her and stopped catching bugs. They waddled to the fence, quacking at her. She threw them the rest of her bread and walked down the path to the ring of shells. She sat down on the rusty iron bench and tried to imagine how this garden had looked long ago.

In the silence, she heard voices. Men's voices.

"It's a big piece of land," one was saying. "You could put at least two houses on it. Clear all this stuff off and clean it up, and get rid of that old ruin."

"But the old lady doesn't want to sell," said the other.

"She'll have no choice," said the first. "It will be sold for taxes, and it ought to go cheap. I've been talking to the neighbors. Next we'll talk to the Town Board and file a complaint. That should speed things up."

"Okay, I'll go along with that."

The footsteps died away and a car door slammed. Maggie sat still, looking around at the remains of the garden and the decrepit house. A ruin, that man had called it. Maybe so, but suddenly she knew she couldn't bear to have it destroyed. Buried under the overgrown vegetation and the mess, the beautiful old place was still there. They would have to do something, and she thought she knew what it was. She hurried back to the house. Grandma was downstairs, drinking coffee.

"Grandma!" Maggie exclaimed. "I just heard something. Some men were outside talking. They want to go to the Town Board, whatever that is, and file a complaint because the house is a mess. They say then Cousin Esther will have to sell her house because she hasn't paid the taxes. So we have to do something."

"What should we do?" Grandma asked. "We can't pay the taxes."

"Well, at least we could clean up the mess," said Maggie.

"It's a good idea," Grandma agreed, "but how are we

going to do it? We can sweep the floor and wash the windows, but we can't fix the loose boards or the porch steps—"

"I can so!" said Maggie. "I know how. Marcus can help me."

"But we can't cart away that heavy junk or fix the driveway or put in new pipes."

Marcus was listening quietly, the way he always did. Suddenly he said, "I know who can."

"Yes? Who?"

"Mr. Ramon."

"Maybe you're right," said Grandma. "That reminds me, I have to call him. I promised to let him know where we are. We must do it right now."

She finished her coffee, quickly combed her hair and smoothed her skirt.

"Get some money out of the teapot," she said.

"There isn't much left," said Maggie.

"I'll have to think of something," Grandma said. "Maybe I'll ask my boss to advance me some money. Trouble is, it'll take a few days to get here. Well, come on. Laurie and Marcus can stay here. They'll be all right with Lucky."

As they drove to the village, Maggie looked about, trying to memorize the appearance of the street, so she would have a picture of it in her mind. It was so pretty. Kids were riding bicycles, playing ball, running with their dogs. She wondered what Marcus would do when they had to part from Lucky.

Grandma must have been thinking the same thing, for she said, "I used to have a dog when I was a kid.

Followed me everywhere. Funny, I haven't thought of him in years. Bonzo."

"What happened to him?"

"He got lost. Or maybe hit by a car. I don't know. I cried for days."

"Grandma," said Maggie, "do you think some kid is crying for Lucky?"

"It could be," said Grandma. She turned into Main Street. There were more cars than there had been yesterday. Grandma got the last parking space in the block.

"Why so many people?" Maggie asked.

"It's morning, and it's Thursday. Must be early closing day. I better get some groceries in."

They went into Hank Duffy's store.

"Morning, Susie," said Hank, grinning from his perch behind the counter. "You leaving? Said you wouldn't stay long."

"No, I'm not leaving," Grandma snapped. "I just want some information. Do buses from the city stop here?"

"Sure they do," said Hank. "You think this is the backwoods?"

"I did think so, seeing you sitting there," said Grandma.

She and Maggie went to the phone booth at the back of the store.

"You dial, Maggie," said Grandma. "I haven't got my glasses."

"You're scared," said Maggie, dialing and putting in the money. She heard the phone ring and then a voice answered.

"Diane!" she said. "It's me, Maggie."

"Maggie!" Diane screamed. "Papa, Mama, it's Maggie!"

Then Mr. Ramon was shouting into the phone. "Where are you? You said you call me right away! Where your grandma?"

"Here, I'll put her on."

"Hello, Mr. Ramon, what's all the excitement?"

"Oh, Miz Miklusky! You don't know what I go through. Some guys come, want to know where is car. I say I don't know, somebody steal her, I say I tell cops. They say no don't tell cops, just want car back. They say they give me a thousand dollars for her. I think they crazy, or else hoods."

"Is that all?"

"No, not all. The lady come, want to know where you at. I don't know. She very mad. She come every day, stay in your house. I go crazy, my wife go crazy."

"Didn't she go to California?"

"No, she wait for you to come back. Then cops come. Want to know where is car. Cops put it on radio. I go nuts."

"But why?"

"Don't know. They don't tell me nothing."

There was the sound of an argument. Then Mrs. Ramon came on.

"Please, Mrs. Miklusky, I am so glad you are okay. We don't hear from you, I think you have accident. Where you are at?"

Grandma said, "Calm down, Mrs. Ramon. We're at my cousin's house. Esther Crouse, her name is. It's in

Mountainside, New York. You write it down. But please don't tell anybody, especially Ruby, you hear?"

"Okay, okay, where that is?"

"It's in the mountains. It's so nice here. The only thing is, my cousin is having a little trouble and we have to help her out."

"When you come home?"

"Pretty soon, Mrs. Ramon. Only please, I want to ask a favor. We need somebody to help us fix a few things. You think your husband could come up for a couple of days? We'll pay him, as soon as I get my next check. He can come on the bus. Maybe bring Diane. Then we'll all drive home together."

"Okay, I ask him. Then I phone you back."

"No, we have no phone. You talk it over, and I'll call you tomorrow." She hung up and they walked out.

"And now," Grandma said, "we'll do our shopping before the stores close. Then I'll try to get my boss."

"Have we got enough money for groceries and gas?"

"If we don't buy too much," said Grandma.

They walked along the street looking into the windows. There was a hardware store with garden tools and barbecue grills.

"We could use some of those things," Maggie said.

There was a real-estate office with pictures of elegant houses for sale.

"Look, Grandma!" said Maggie. "Here's one for sixty thousand dollars! Does anybody have that much money?"

"Only rich people," said Grandma.

They passed a shop with ladies' clothes.

"That would look good on you," said Maggie, pointing to a pair of bright yellow shorts and a matching T-shirt.

Next door to that was an art shop. Marcus would like some of those paints and brushes, Maggie thought. She admired some framed pictures in the window, especially one of a garden full of flowers, with a pond and a weeping willow, in a carved and gilded frame like the one she had seen in the attic. She wondered how much it was, and whether Cousin Esther could sell hers.

At last they got to the grocery store, passing the doughnut shop on the way. Grandma paused in front of the doughnut shop.

"Come on, Grandma," Maggie urged, pulling her sleeve. Grandma came on, but she appeared to be thinking hard about something.

They bought dog food, hamburger and rolls, milk and fruit. Grandma passed up potato chips in favor of a sack of potatoes, and she promised to make cookies rather than buy them. Then they started back to the car. But suddenly in front of the doughnut shop, she stopped.

"You go sit in the car," she said. "I have to see about something." And she hurried into the doughnut shop.

Maggie waited nervously. Why was Grandma going to buy doughnuts when she had just said they had to economize? Fifteen minutes went by. What was going on? She was about to go in and see, when Grandma appeared, smiling with satisfaction, and carrying a big bag of doughnuts.

She plumped herself into the car and started the motor. She drove around the corner to the gas station.

"Fill her up!" she ordered.

"Grandma!" said Maggie. "I thought we were broke!"

"Ha!" said Grandma. "I just got a job in the doughnut shop. Told 'em I could make a better doughnut than the ones they have. I start tomorrow. Now come on home."

They drove home at high speed. Cousin Esther wasn't home yet, but Marcus and Laurie were sitting on the porch steps looking very angry and upset. Laurie had been crying, and Marcus had a tight hold on Lucky's rope.

"Some boys came to dig in the yard," Marcus said. Marcus had told them to go away and Lucky had barked. So they went, but they said mean things. They said people didn't like all the junk that Esther piled up, and she would have to move. Then a man came and said to tell Esther that keeping ducks was against the law. Marcus said he wouldn't tell her anything like that. They didn't know where Maggie and Grandma were, and they were feeling scared.

"You'll feel better after lunch," said Grandma. "Don't worry about those people."

Maggie cooked hamburgers, after which Grandma decided to go back to the village and do some wash in the Laundromat.

"You kids behave yourselves and I'll bring something good for supper," she said. "Tomorrow I'll phone Mr. Ramon again, and maybe he'll come out and give us a hand." And she was off.

Left to themselves, Maggie, Marcus and Laurie sat on the top step of the porch. It was a lovely afternoon, just like the beautiful day when they had all gone on a picnic beside the river. That had been fun, and they had been so happy and carefree! And they could have had fun today too, if only they hadn't so many worries.

"I wish we could stay here always," said Marcus. "I don't wanna go back to the city."

"Me too," said Laurie. "I wanna stay here and play with the kitties and help Grandma and Cousin Esther."

Maggie said, "But maybe Cousin Esther won't even be here. She might have to sell the house because she can't afford to pay the taxes. And we have to give the car back to Mr. Ramon, and Aunt Ruby hasn't gone to California after all. She's just waiting for us to come back so she can get us."

"You better not go back," said Marcus. "I wonder how much the taxes are. Do you think they're more than three hundred dollars?"

"I don't know," said Maggie. "Why?"

"Well," said Marcus, unwillingly, "I could give Lucky back. I could call up those people and ask them if they want her. I don't think her name is really Josephine, but maybe it is."

Maggie said, "Gee, Marcus, do you really mean it?"

"Yes, I mean it," said Marcus. "I don't want to but I'll do it."

"We could write them a letter," Maggie said. "That's cheaper than phoning."

"Okay," said Marcus, grimly. He got up and went inside. He came back with the drawing pad Grandma had bought and one of his Magic Markers. He sat down and wrote:

To the people who lost a dog:

    We have a dog like yours. We found her on the Taconic Parkway last week. We like her very much but if she is yours, you can have her if you will pay the $300. We need it to pay the taxes.

                Write to Mrs. Susan Miklusky
                % Esther Crouse
                Mountainside, N.Y.

"I thought I better put Grandma's name," he explained.

"That's a good letter," said Maggie. "Now you need an envelope and a stamp. When Grandma comes back we'll ask her to take us to the post office."

"If I had any money," Marcus said, "I'd mail it right now. Then I'd surprise Grandma."

Maggie dug in the pocket of her jeans. There was the change from the groceries.

"Take it," she said. "You can walk to the village. It isn't too far. Take Lucky with you."

Marcus started off, and Maggie and Laurie went back into the house. Maggie washed the dishes. Then they took the blankets and sheets out on the porch to air.

"Watch out, don't trip on that loose board," Maggie said. "You know what, I'm going to fix it right now. Go get that hammer Marcus brought along."

Laurie brought the hammer and Maggie rummaged in a drawer and found some nails. Soon she was down on her knees driving them into the floor.

"One of those porch steps is wobbly," she said as she

banged. "I'll fix that too while I'm at it. Only I can't fix that roof," she admitted reluctantly.

Next they decided to wash the kitchen windows. Laurie washed the lower panes and Maggie did the upper ones. They tidied the living room and stacked the books and magazines.

"You know what I wish?" said Maggie. "I wish Diane was here. She'd help fix this place up. Maybe Mr. Ramon will bring her."

They were so busy that they didn't have time to feel downcast. Suddenly they heard the rattle and clatter of Cousin Esther's car in the driveway. Looking out of the window, they saw Marcus, Lucky and Esther getting out of the car. Esther had caught up with them and actually given them a ride! She and Marcus were talking. Even more remarkable, Esther bent down and patted Lucky on the head, and Lucky reached up and licked her nose!

"You know what?" said Maggie. "She likes Lucky!"

"Who doesn't?" said Laurie.

Cousin Esther's good mood lasted. She praised Maggie and said the living room looked better than it had in months. She said Marcus was a good kid for writing the letter, but she hoped those people weren't the real owners of Lucky. She showed Laurie how to wind up the phonograph and start it playing, and said she was the only kid she had ever seen who knew how to handle a kitten.

By the time Grandma came home they were getting along like a house afire. Grandma marched in carrying a big flat box.

"I brought a pizza for our supper," she said. "I'm starved. And here's some ice cream. Put it in the refrigerator quick before it melts."

"Grandma!" said Maggie. "There's no refrigerator!"

"Oh, I forgot. Well, we'll have to eat it fast."

"What got into *you*?" Cousin Esther asked.

"Oh, didn't you know? I got a job making doughnuts," said Grandma. "Four dollars an hour and all the doughnuts I want, starting tomorrow. The laundry is in the car. Marcus, you get it."

Supper was a gay meal. They ate in the dining room, and afterward sat in the living room listening to records.

Suddenly they were surprised to hear Laurie singing along with the record:

> Maxwelton's braes are bonnie
> Where early falls the dew,
> And it's there that Annie Laurie
> Gave me her promise true.

Both Grandma and Esther exclaimed, "Where'd you learn that song?"

"My dad used to sing it," Laurie said. "That's my name, Annie Laurie. Mom doesn't like it."

"Why did she name you that, then?" Maggie asked.

"Oh, she's not my real mother," said Laurie.

That depressed them all for a while. But then Maggie rummaged through the stack of records and found "Clementine," and they all sang that with great gusto. Even Marcus cheered up and almost forgot the letter he had written.

Esther said, "This is the best evening I've had in ten years."

As they took their candles and went off to bed, Maggie whispered, "I think she likes having us here."

"Yes," Grandma said. "It's good for her. But it isn't enough. It's going to take something special to save this place. Well, don't worry. We'll think of something."

Friday morning, Grandma had no time to sit and think. As soon as breakfast was over, she hurried off to the village. Cousin Esther went off to work too, leaving the children to keep themselves occupied. It was a little scary, being left on their own.

"It's so quiet here," Marcus complained.

Maggie decided the best thing was to keep busy. She found some big plastic bags and they began picking up cans and bottles and papers.

"Don't cut yourself," she warned. "Grandma will take that stuff to the dump in the wagon."

"You kids did a good job," Cousin Esther said when she got home. And Grandma nodded approvingly.

"I brought barbecued chicken for supper, and an apple pie. Getting a little tired of doughnuts."

"Did you call Mr. Ramon?"

"Yes, I did," said Grandma. "I didn't get any sense out of him, though."

She explained that she had dialed the number and Mrs. Ramon answered. Grandma was about to ask whether Mr. Ramon could come, and to give him directions, when there was a crashing noise and the connection was broken.

"They hung up," she said. "I don't know what happened. I rang again and there was no answer. I'll try again tomorrow."

"Did you call your boss?"

"Yes. He said I could stay out another week. He misses me, though. Says the customers are complaining." She looked pleased.

Saturday was much like Friday. By afternoon there was a whole row of plastic bags ready to be taken away. The yard was somewhat cleaner but the children were dirty.

"Tonight you kids have baths," said Grandma. "Tomorrow we all take a rest."

"If only Diane were here," said Maggie. "Did you get Mr. Ramon?"

"No. Tried twice, and no answer," said Grandma. "I can't understand it."

ELEVEN

It was Sunday.

"This is very nice," said Grandma, sitting at the breakfast table and pouring herself another cup of coffee.

The sun streamed in through the newly washed windows. Breakfast had been a leisurely meal. They had eaten pancakes with syrup and bacon until they couldn't hold any more, and Lucky and the ducks had to finish up what was left.

Laurie was playing on the floor with the kittens. Marcus was drawing a picture of the kitchen with the group at the table. Maggie was composing a letter to Diane.

Dear Diane:

   I really wish you were here. You and Pedro.
I miss you both. This is such a nice place and
we could have fun fixing it up. It would be
more fun than the dollhouse. I love it and wish
I could stay here forever.

   She was going to give the letter to Mr. Ramon when
he came, which they all hoped would be soon. She had
reminded Grandma about phoning him.

   "I tried to get him twice yesterday," Grandma said.
"But there was no answer. We'll try again today. Don't
worry."

   Maggie put her letter down and started to put the
dishes in the sink, but Esther said, "Sit down, Maggie,
and take it easy awhile."

   "Should we go to the village and buy a paper?"
Maggie asked.

   "Oh, what for?" said Grandma. "We don't need to
read any bad news. Really, Esther, I think you are right
not to have any radios or TV in the house. It's very
relaxing not to know what's going on. Just think, if we
hadn't seen that paper, Marcus would never know that
people were advertising for Lucky, and he'd be perfectly
happy."

   Maggie thought, but then we wouldn't get the three-
hundred-dollar reward. However, it did not seem tactful
to say it aloud. And it *was* nice not hearing about the
old black car with the wrong license plates. She was so
used to the green car now that she had almost forgotten
it used to be black.

"I'm taking Lucky for a walk," Marcus said.

Maggie got up to go with him. She stood on the porch for a moment and smelled the cool morning air. It was very quiet. There was no sound but the birds in the trees, and a far-off church bell ringing, and now and then a car going by.

They walked down the driveway, past Esther's old car and the bright green station wagon.

"Hey! Look at that!" Maggie exclaimed. "A flat tire!"

The right rear tire had obviously gone over a nail or piece of glass. It was very flat.

"We can't go anywhere till it's fixed," said Marcus. "And Cousin Esther can't move her car because ours is in the way."

They ran back to report the news.

"Drat it!" said Grandma. "Spoiling a nice Sunday morning like this! Somebody will have to walk down to the garage. Esther, it wouldn't hurt to have a phone in the house. Soon as I make some more money I'll get one."

"Don't need it," said Esther. "Don't need the garage either. Closed on Sunday anyhow. I can change a tire. Done it often. Come on."

They tramped down to the car.

"Where's the jack?" Esther asked. "And the spare?"

"I don't know," said Grandma. "Never needed them before."

"Must be in the back," said Esther, opening the tailgate. She lifted the floor of the car, and there underneath was the spare tire, the jack and a wrench.

And something more. When they had lifted out the tools, and wrestled out the tire, they saw at the bottom a pair of license plates. The number on them was 303-NM2.

Speechless, they stared at the plates. What did it mean?

Finally Grandma spoke. "It really *is* the get-away car," she whispered.

"So that's what the cops were looking for!" said Esther. "Well, come on, we got to change the tire, no matter what."

But Maggie said, "Wait."

There was something else. Stuffed into a corner of the tire well was a bundle of rags. She pulled it out. It was heavy and knobby. She unwrapped the rags, layer after layer, until she came to a canvas bag tied at the top with a string.

She peered inside. Then, spreading out the rags on the tailgate, she poured out a stream of rings, pins, watches, chains, bracelets, all encrusted with diamonds and other sparkling stones.

"It's the loot!" Grandma breathed. "From the jewelry store. So that's why the thieves wanted to get the car back. They offered Mr. Ramon a thousand dollars for it."

"Aren't they pretty!" said Esther, picking up a bracelet and trying it on. "I always wanted a diamond bracelet."

"Goes good with that flannel shirt of yours," said Grandma. "You put that back, Esther Crouse, and Maggie, take that bag and those plates into the house and hide them somewhere. Soon as we get this tire changed we're off to the police."

Maggie ran as if the police were already after her.

She rushed into the house and looked around frantically. Then her eye lit on the big black stove. She opened the oven, shoved the loot and the plates as far back as possible, and piled an assortment of pots and pans in front. Then she ran out again.

Esther was struggling with the wrench, trying to unscrew the nuts on the flat tire.

"Never saw things so hard to move," she puffed. "Must be rusted on."

"Esther," said Grandma, "for goodness sake give it up. We'll get a man from the garage. You'll bust yourself doing that."

A boy's voice said, "Can I help you, lady?"

Maggie looked around at the boy who stood there, and screamed, "Pedro!" She threw her arms around his neck.

Then, blushing as red as a beet she stepped back and muttered, "How the heck did you get here?"

Pedro grinned and pointed to the street. A pickup truck stood there. Climbing out of it were Tom and Mary Ann.

"Esther," said Grandma, "these are the young people we stayed with, and this is Pedro, who came from the city with us. What a surprise!"

Mary Ann said, "Pedro was worried about you. I think he missed Maggie." (It was now Pedro's turn to get red.) "And we were wondering too, so we took the day off and came to see."

"But how did you know where to come?" Maggie asked.

"Mountainside isn't so big," said Mary Ann. "We just

asked at the paper store if they knew a lady named Mrs. Miklusky with three children and a dog, and the man said, 'Oh, you mean Susie? She's visiting her cousin Esther Crouse.' So here we are."

"Just in time too," said Grandma. "Esther was about to kill herself changing a tire."

"That's man's work," said Tom. He and Pedro and Marcus got to work. In about ten minutes the wheel was changed. "What else can we do for you?" Tom asked. Then he explained to Esther, "These folks did so much for us, we can never repay them. We've got a house, a business, and a boy. His folks said he could stay with us till we got tired of him. So far we haven't."

"We better all go inside," said Esther. "The neighbors will think you're buying the place."

As they walked up the driveway Tom and Mary Ann gazed around in amazement.

"I wouldn't mind buying it if I had any money," said Tom. "This house is a beauty. A real antique!"

"You tell that to the neighbors," said Esther. "They want to tear it down."

"What! They're crazy!" yelled Tom. "Show me the inside."

But before they could get inside, a horn tooted loudly. Somebody else had arrived. A car had entered the driveway and the driver, finding there was no room, was trying to back out again and was stuck on one of the rocks in the driveway.

"Who's that?" Esther demanded crossly. "Whoever they are, they don't know how to drive. Out! Out!" she shouted. "No room!"

The driver stuck his head out and shouted back, "Mrs. Miklusky! We look for Mrs. Miklusky!"

"It's Mr. Ramon!" Grandma shrieked.

"Diane! Diane!" Maggie screamed as another head appeared. She rushed down the driveway. Then she stopped in horror. In the car, besides Mr. and Mrs. Ramon and Diane, was Aunt Ruby.

Maggie ran back. "Grandma!" she whispered. "Aunt Ruby is here."

"Ruby!" said Grandma. "What's she doing here? You mean the Ramons brought her? I'll fix them." And she walked down to the car with her hands on her hips.

"Hello, Mr. Ramon," she said. "Where'd you get the car?"

Mr. Ramon, his face contorted with worry and frustration, climbed out of the car. "I explain everything," he said between clenched teeth. "That lady there, she drive me crazy. She rent car, she pay for everything, she make me come here. You better talk to her."

He was obviously about to explode. Grandma sized up the situation.

"Well, Ruby," she said, "what a surprise to see you here! Come on in, everybody, so Mr. Ramon can get his car straightened out. Tom! Where's Tom? Oh, here you are. Will you help Mr. Ramon?"

And she herded the whole group into the house, leaving the two men to sort things out.

"Don't worry, Tom will calm him down," she said to Mrs. Ramon, who was almost in tears.

Maggie and Diane hugged each other joyfully. "Oh, I missed you so much," Maggie said. "I had so much to tell you. And look, Pedro is here. Isn't that great?"

Diane said, "I wanted to see you so much, sometimes I cried."

They were interrupted by Aunt Ruby, who was picking her way over the stones with a sour look on her face. "Well, Margaret Agnes," she said, "I waited for you to come back to the city but you didn't come. So I had to come to see you."

Maggie wanted to say that that wasn't at all necessary, but it would not have been polite. So she said. "Well, we were coming back but Cousin Esther needed us to help her with some problems. There's a lot to do here."

Aunt Ruby looked around and said, "Yes, I can see that."

They went into the house with the others, and all crowded into the kitchen. Lucky, seeing Pedro and Mary Ann, barked and almost went mad with joy. The cats and kittens, however, horrified by the invasion, ran for their lives and hid under the couch.

Grandma began to make more coffee, and Maggie got out cups and spoons. Fortunately there were lots of doughnuts.

"Grandma made them," she boasted.

Mrs. Ramon said, "Oh, I make a big pot of chili. Pedro, go tell Ramon to bring from car."

"Oh, boy, chili!" said Pedro. "I haven't had any in almost a week."

Mary Ann laughed. "Pedro is trying to teach me to make it. If I can learn how, maybe he'll be happy in our house."

The kitchen was crammed with people, all shouting at once. They were joined by Mr. Ramon and Tom, who were loaded down with chili, cake, fruit, tacos and wine.

Mr. Ramon was excited. "Mrs. Crouse," he said, bowing, "you have a beautiful place here. So many trees, bushes, vines. Is like my home in Puerto Rico, like the jungle." He set his load down and went to the back door. "And here are ducks! Real ducks! And more trees. You have garden? No? I would like to dig for you."

Mrs. Ramon scolded him. "Keep still, Ramon, you are talking too much. Sit down and take a rest now."

Cousin Esther thought they should all sit down. "There's chairs in the dining room," she said. "You boys go get them. My! Twelve people! Haven't been so many since Papa was alive!" Her frizzy hair shook with unaccustomed excitement.

At last they were all crowded around the kitchen table. Grandma poured coffee, Laura passed doughnuts, and Maggie brought soda for the children. For a few minutes it was quiet as everyone ate and drank.

Then Grandma said, "Now tell me—"

And Mr. Ramon said, "Please explain—"

And Pedro and Maggie and Diane all burst out, "How come—"

They all began to talk at once. Grandma banged on the table.

"One at a time," she shouted. "Mr. Ramon first. How come you're driving a car when I thought you were coming on the bus?"

Little by little things were cleared up. Aunt Ruby had been there Thursday when Grandma telephoned. She had looked over Mrs. Ramon's shoulder and seen

Cousin Esther's address. She at once took charge, rented a car, and insisted on starting Saturday afternoon, making Mr. Ramon do the driving. She had got maps and figured out how to go. They had stayed at a motel overnight, so as to get to Mountainside on Sunday morning. Her doctor friend had gone on to California, and Aunt Ruby would join him as soon as she got everything squared away.

"Now this is my plan," she began. And then she sneezed.

Mr. Ramon had other things on his mind. "Where is my black station wagon?" he wanted to know.

"Kachoo! Kachoo!" went Aunt Ruby.

"Why, it's right out there," said Maggie, "Only we painted it green. We kept hearing that they were looking for a black wagon. Even though they gave the wrong license number, people were giving us funny looks. So Tom and Mary Ann helped us paint it. Only we couldn't understand why they wanted it. Now we know."

"You know?" Mr. Ramon asked. "What do you know?"

"Can I tell, Grandma?" Maggie asked.

Grandma nodded. Maggie got up, went to the stove and opened the oven door. She pulled out the pots and pans, and then the license plates and the canvas bag wrapped in rags.

"We had a flat tire," she said. "We took the spare out of the car, and underneath we found these things."

Then, as before, she poured out the shining treasure in the middle of the table, among the coffee cups.

"Kachoo!" sneezed Aunt Ruby, wiping her eyes.

"It's the loot!" Mr. Ramon exploded. "Holy Mary save us! You found it! That's why they look for car. First the *ladrónes*, the robbers, they leave it in the garage. Then some of them get arrested. They are in jail. The others want to get the car but meanwhile I buy it. I get new plates. They want to get it back from me but they don't tell why. And I don't tell them Mrs. Miklusky take it for a trip. She tell me not to say. So I tell to them that it is stolen."

"But somebody must have told the cops that the stuff was in the car," said Maggie. "Who did that?"

"You know who? Marcus' uncle. He's in jail. Because is the same bunch that robbed the TV store. That's when he gets caught. Now he spills the *frijoles*."

"Spills the beans, Papa," said Diane.

"Okay, okay, beans. What's difference?"

Marcus said, "I guess he's not such a bad guy after all. But I still wish I didn't have to go back and live with him."

"Don't worry, Marcus," said Mrs. Ramon. "You will not go to him. He sent a message. He say if you can stay with Mrs. Miklusky, that will be best for you."

Marcus smiled. A great load was lifted from his shoulders, and he sat up straight and said, "Is it okay with you, Grandma?"

"It's okay," said Grandma.

"But what about me?" Laurie asked. "Is there a message for me?"

"No. No message," said Mrs. Ramon. "Your mother, she went someplace and didn't come back. *Pobre niña!*

I think she deserted you. What kind of a mother is that?"

Maggie said, "She's not her real mother."

Laurie looked up at Grandma. "I don't mind, if you'll be my real grandmother."

Grandma put her arms around Laurie. "Of course I will. Only you can't have more than three cats at a time."

"I don't need cats if I have you and Maggie," Laurie said.

"Kachoo! Kachoo! Cats!" exclaimed Aunt Ruby.

"Ruby, what *is* the matter with you?" Grandma asked. "Have you got a cold?"

"No!" Aunt Ruby said. "It's the cats. I'm allergic. I better go outside." And she walked out, blowing her nose and wiping her eyes.

Grandma looked at Maggie. "Who would have thought it?" she exclaimed. "We didn't know how to deal with Ruby, and all we needed was a couple of cats! Poor Ruby! Now folks," she went on, addressing the entire group. "we have to decide a few things. Esther here needs a little help with her house, and I thought—"

But Cousin Esther interrupted.

"Susie, you always were a great one for butting in. You may not like the way I do things but it's my house, and if I choose to sell it or let it fall down that's my business."

Grandma looked a little abashed for a moment but quickly recovered herself. "Why, Esther," she said, "It's all right with me if you want to sell it to some real-estate sharks or let it fall down, but before you do, I thought you would do me a favor. See, I have these kids here, Marcus and Laurie, plus this dog, and I thought when I go back to the city, to my job, you know, maybe you'd board them for me for a few weeks. Of course I'd take Maggie with me."

"Grandma!" Maggie cried. "That's not fair! I want to stay here!"

Grandma's eyes twinkled. "See? Now she wants to desert me. Maybe I better stay and keep them in order. If you'll have me, that is."

Esther sniffed. "Looks like you better stay here so Maggie can keep *you* in order."

Mr. Ramon had been waiting for a chance to talk. Now he burst out: "How I wish I can stay too. I could fix everything for you. Fix the pipes, the porch roof, the garden."

Tom had been walking around the house looking up at the window frames, the paneling, the carved woodwork and the oak floors. He came back to the table.

"This house shouldn't just be fixed. It should be restored. If we only knew what it used to look like."

"I know," said Maggie. "There's a picture in the attic. Cousin Esther, can I show them?"

"Sure," said Esther. "Everybody can go. Take a flashlight, there's no light up there." The whole party tramped up the strairs. In the attic Maggie uncovered the painting.

"Isn't this how it looked?" Maggie asked.

"Yes, my sister Bertha painted that a long time ago. Take it down if you want."

But Tom was poking around among the piled-up furniture.

"Where did all this stuff come from?" he asked, examining a chair, a chest of drawers and a gateleg table.

Esther said, "Oh, this is old family stuff. Mama got tired of it and bought a set of golden oak. We never threw it out—we just stuck it up here."

"It's priceless!" said Tom. "You could sell it for quite a lot."

"Don't know who would buy this old junk," said Esther doubtfully.

"I know," said Mary Ann. "That woman at our sale who made such a fuss because we had no more antiques."

They trooped downstairs with the painting and two of the chairs.

"Esther," said Grandma, as they passed the cluttered bedrooms, "what in the name of common sense are you keeping all this junk for?"

"Folks give me stuff," said Esther. "I can't use it. I was going to give it to the Salvation Army only I was busy."

Mary Ann cried, "No! Don't do that! Have a yard sale! We had one and it was great! We'll help you."

"Got to clear up the yard first," said Esther.

"Now folks," said Grandma as they crowded into the kitchen again, "I propose we eat and then do something with the loot—where is the loot? It's gone!"

"Don't worry, Grandma," said Maggie. "I put it away."

"I don't know what I'd do without that girl," said Grandma.

"You will get reward," Mr. Ramon said. "The jewelry store offers two thousand dollars."

"But that's yours," said Grandma. "It's your car."

"But you find," said Mr. Ramon. "If not for you, I would sell the car back to the *ladrónes*. So is yours. But I make a deal. I come out and fix the house, I fix yard, everything, if you let us come out for weekends in the country."

"Oh, yes!" Mrs. Ramon said. "Is so good to breathe fresh air and see green trees growing."

"We'll divide it fifty–fifty," said Grandma. "That's my last word."

Tom, carrying the painting, walked out on the porch. "Let's see what the outside looked like—" he began.

But there, an unexpected sight met their eyes.

Aunt Ruby, standing at the top of the steps, was glaring down at two men who stood there.

"No, you will not come in," she said sternly. "I don't care who you are. Miss Crouse has guests and is busy. You may give me that paper. I will see that it is delivered."

"But ma'am, it's a summons," said one man. "I have to give it to her personally."

"Come back some other time, then," said Aunt Ruby. "Go on, now!"

The two men turned and walked away, muttering something about interfering with the law.

"That's that," she said, dusting her hands together. Then she turned and addressed the group standing just inside the door.

"I won't come in," she said severely. "The cat hairs in there would bring on my asthma. But I have something to say, so will you please come out? Margaret Agnes, come here."

Maggie approached timidly, looking back at Grandma for help.

"I have been looking over the situation here," she said. "I talked to some children who came by. You may know them, a blonde girl and a dark-haired one. They seem like nice children. They were on their way to Sunday School. This seems like a respectable neighborhood, much better than that slum you live in now."

"It isn't—" Maggie began.

"Wait. I have not finished. If you and your grandmother should decide to move out to this village, so that you can go to school here, my mind will be at ease."

"But Aunt Ruby!" Maggie exclaimed. "That's just what we want to do. Cousin Esther will let us stay here, and we're going to fix up the house and here's what it used to look like and Mr. Ramon will help, and— Oh, it's wonderful!" And she threw her arms around Aunt Ruby and kissed her.

As this was the first time Maggie had ever done such a thing, Aunt Ruby was struck dumb. She looked amazed, then her face cracked into a sort of smile, and she awkwardly patted Maggie on the head.

"Well, well!" she said. "I also wanted to say that I'll be glad to help financially. I *was* going to take care of you in California, so if you don't mind—"

Grandma said, "Well, Ruby, that's very kind of you. But I already have a job here, and there's the reward money, and Esther's furniture will take care of her, so thanks very much just the same."

Mrs. Ramon now announced that her pot of chili needed to be heated and she didn't know how to make a fire in that stove with all the jewelry in it.

"No, no!" Maggie shrieked, running to the kitchen to light the oil stove. Diane came too.

"Oh, Diane!" Maggie said, hugging her friend. "It's going to be such fun! We'll have a house! A real house! I mean it's Cousin Esther's but she'll let us stay and fix it up and you can come out and help. And I'll really do carpentry—and everything!"

"Yeah! And Pedro can come and see us sometimes," Diane said, grinning.

As Aunt Ruby was afraid to go back into the house, they carried a table and chairs outside. Tom went to the village for some ice.

"Now the first thing you had better buy is a refrigerator," Aunt Ruby said. "I can't have my niece getting ptomaine from spoiled food."

Grandma opened her mouth to let fly with a sharp retort when Maggie poked her and she closed it again.

"I will gladly pay for one," said Aunt Ruby, "if you'll allow me to, of course."

"First thing is to pay the light bill and get the electric again," Esther muttered.

At last all the food was consumed except a small amount of chili in the bottom of the pot.

"Here, Pedro, you finish it," said Maggie.

"I give you recipe," Mrs. Ramon promised Mary Ann.

It was time to go. Tom loaded two of Esther's old chairs into his pickup to show to the disappointed lady.

"And mind you put a good price on them," Grandma warned.

Aunt Ruby and the Ramons walked to the rented car which was out by the curb. Diane was staying behind.

"Good-bye, Maggie," said Aunt Ruby. It was the first time she had called her anything but Margaret Agnes.

"Good-bye, Aunt Ruby," said Maggie. "And if you want, I'll come and see you in California."

Aunt Ruby was speechless again. She stood there smiling, not sure how to reply. Finally she said, "Morris and I will be very happy to have you. And your grandmother too, of course." And she leaned forward and gave Maggie a peck on the cheek.

"Write to us, Ruby," Grandma called. "Tell us how it is out there."

With all this kissing going on, Pedro climbed quickly into the Allens' truck. "So long, kids," he called. "I'll be seeing you."

Grandma, Esther, Maggie, Diane, Laurie and Marcus were left behind. They stood at the curb waving till their friends' cars were out of sight. Lucky sat watching beside Marcus, her tongue hanging out in a cheerful grin.

Two girls came toward them.

"Hi, Miss Crouse," said Liz. "We just heard your friends are staying."

"That's right," said Esther.

"We're glad," said Judy. "They look like good kids."

"How did they know?" Maggie asked when they had passed.

"I told you, out here everybody knows everything," said Grandma.

"They looked nice," Diane observed.

"Yes, out here most folks are nice." They turned and started back to the house, tired but happy. That is, everybody was happy except Marcus. He scowled gloomily.

"What's wrong, Marcus?" Grandma asked.

"Oh nothing," he grumbled, "only I wish those people would answer my letter."

"Today is Sunday," said Maggie. "No mail on Sunday."

But just then a horn tooted. A red, white and blue truck had stopped. "Special delivery for Mrs. Miklusky," the driver said.

"For me?" said Grandma. She tore open the letter.

"Dear Madam," she read. "With reference to the dog found on the parkway, we would like to inform you that the dog stolen from our home had a tattoo mark behind its left front leg. The number is 765432. If the dog you have found bears that number, it is ours and we will gladly come and get it and pay the reward. Please call us collect in any case."

Marcus looked as if he was about to faint.

"Lucky!" he said. "Come here!"

He tried to look behind her left front leg but the thick wool got in the way.

"I can't," he said. "Somebody help."

Maggie said, "She has to lie down and roll over." Lying on her back with all four legs waving in the air, Lucky looked very silly. What kind of new game is this? she seemed to be wondering.

Maggie parted the hair and looked. They all looked all over Lucky's stomach. She didn't mind being tickled but what was the matter with these humans?

"There's nothing there," Maggie finally pronounced. "She's somebody else."

It was too much for Marcus. He threw himself on top of Lucky and began to cry while she licked the tears away.

"What's he crying for?" Laurie asked.

"That's what is called crying for joy," said Grandma. "Come on, let's give him five minutes. Then we have to go to town to phone. First the police and then the people with the lost dog. And after that—"

"You'll think of something," Esther grumbled.

ELEANOR CLYMER once asked a group of ten-, eleven-, and twelve-year-olds what they most liked to read and write. Their unanimous answer was mystery, adventure, and humor. In writing *The Get-away Car,* she must have shared their outlook. As she formed the characters, she said, "I didn't try to make them too credible. I just wanted the story to gallop along amusingly.

"Although Grandma and her entourage are all fictitious, the car they borrowed was modeled on one my husband and I bought years ago for ten dollars. We found it at a garage where it had been left by some gangsters!"

Mrs. Clymer has written numerous children's books. She and her husband live in Katonah, New York.